Pandora's Box
A series: book 3

V.M. JACKSON

PANDORA'S BOX

PANDORA'S BOX is a work of fiction. The events and characters that are described are imaginary and are not intended to refer to specific places or living persons.

Chapter 1

Taken

Junior year of high school; Virginia Beach, Virginia, 1999

"I'm pregnant," Pandora's voice cracked. She tried to swallow the growing lump in her throat as she watched a second blue line appear on the pregnancy test in her hand.

Bruce felt his stomach do a free fall into his ankles. "Maybe you did it wrong." Grabbing the pregnancy test from his girlfriend, he shook it eagerly hoping one of the lines would disappear. *It didn't.* "It's probably just defective, that's all. Go get another one."

Tears welled up in Pandora's baby brown eyes as she shook her head in denial. "I haven't had my period for almost two months now, and I've been sick for the last three weeks. I'm not stealing another pregnancy test from Mr. Burton's pharmacy to confirm what I *already* know."

The small town of Virginia Beach was a treasure trove of great food, warm hospitality, immense history, and southern charm. It was also a nosey town where everybody knew everything about everyone. They knew your wild big brother and whoring little sister. They knew all about your uncle in rehab for his cocaine addiction and your second cousin who was never quite right after his mother was sent upstate for welfare fraud. Small towns made it extremely awkward to get condoms and impossible to buy a pregnancy test. Unless of course, you wanted your parents to hear about it before you even had the chance to pee on the stick. Bruce lowered his head and used his fingers to pinch the bridge of his nose.

"I'm so sorry, Bruce." Disappointment filled Pandora's eyes as she began to cry.

The Penny Pack Community Park where they stood used to be a peaceful place where Pandora and Bruce did homework and made out after school. They'd watch the birds scavenge for bread and laugh at the innocent children as they frolicked in the green grass. It was such a heavenly atmosphere. Today, it felt like the gates of hell had opened.

Bruce was the number one running back in the country for high school football. He and his best friend Andre, who'd just been named All American for the second year in a row as a Quarterback, were destined for greatness. Alabama University, Clemson, Ohio, and Mississippi had been scouting them since the tenth grade and there was nothing standing in the way of Bruce accepting an offer come senior year— until today.

"Hey…come here," he winced, pulling Pandora's petite body into his chocolate, chiseled arms. "Don't do that. You know I hate it when you cry."

"I feel like I just ruined your life," she muttered in remorse.

This is more my fault than hers, he thought as he stared into the Virginia blue sky with a pensive expression. *This was my stupidity. My horniness. A baby. Screw me.*

Caressing her back, Bruce reached down and kissed the top of Pandora's head in an attempt to comfort her. He was scared out of his mind but he couldn't even begin to imagine what she was going through in her own reality. Reaching down, he lifted her chin so he could look into her eyes. "Stop that. You didn't ruin anything. I was there too, remember?" He grinned.

That comment softened Pandora's expression as a soft giggle escaped her lips. "Yeah. It was a good night."

"It was an *amazing* night," Bruce confirmed, gently wiping away Pandora's remaining tears. It wasn't their first time— or their twentieth, but it was one of their best. The kind they would never forget.

A full moon glistened over the Virginia ocean and the stars gave off just the right amount of light on the dark beach. Soft music floated out of Bruce's dad's 1990 pickup truck as they lay on an oversized blanket in the sand. Soft kisses, hot whispers, sweaty bodies, and grasping hands joined together so deeply that Bruce couldn't tell where she ended, and Pandora couldn't tell where he began. The pleasure was so intense he wanted it to last forever, and she prayed out loud that it would.

Bruce first noticed Pandora in the third grade. He put a frog in her lunch box after Andre dared him too. For a month straight, Pandora tripped Bruce in line and shot spitballs at the back of his head in retribution. By fourth grade, Bruce thought he'd fallen in love with her, and by fifth grade, he was one hundred percent sure of it even though they hadn't formally met yet.

Pandora was sassy, beautiful, and could throw a football better than some of the boys on the football team. In ninth grade, Bruce begged Quinn to introduce them and they became a couple after she circled *yes* on the playful note he passed asking her to be his girlfriend. Three months later she dumped him after Rose Marie Winters offered to let him touch her breasts behind the soda machine in the cafeteria. *And he did.* That summer, they were back together after Bruce won Pandora a teddy bear at the state fair. They were more than just a first crush and a first kiss; they were the best of friends. Junior year of high school hadn't changed anything. Being a handsome star athlete brought Bruce a lot of attention from the ladies, but he only had eyes for Pandora. And as the leader of the debate team, student council, and junior class president, Pandora was quite popular herself. She was lively, bold, and full of spirit. There was a confidence etched in her walk. Her milkshake brought all the little boys to the yard when she pranced by, but they knew not to stare too long out of fear of what Bruce might have done to them. Bruce and Pandora were so absorbed and in love, you couldn't tell them *anything*.

"I'm just gonna go over to the next town and get an abortion."

"No!" His eyes nearly distended out of his sockets. "Are you crazy? My aunt did that back in college and she's never been able to have kids since. She told me that was the biggest regret of her life and to be very careful making selfish decisions like that."

"Bruce, please tell me how we're gonna take care of a baby with no money, job, or place of our own?" She pulled away from him and sat down at a nearby park bench.

"I have no idea, but there has to be a better option than killing it. Maybe my mom and grandma can take care of it. They take care of my sister's kids. I'm sure they wouldn't mind another."

"If we have this baby it'll be our responsibility. We can't just lend it to people to borrow like a pencil," she reared her head back and folded her arms at his audacity. "And what about next year? While everybody is getting ready for senior prom and graduation, we'll be caring for a baby. And what about college? We can't bring a baby to a dorm room! That's ridicu-" Bruce walked over and planted a kiss on her lips, silencing her motor mouth. Sitting down beside her, he pulled her into his lap.

"Just, *shh*, for one second, okay? I don't know what we're gonna do or how we're gonna do it. I'm not ready to be a father and I'm a little afraid of a future I use to be excited about. But we started this and my dad raised me to finish things, not give up and pretend like they never happened.

"But you have your *whole* life ahead of you. I don't want to hold you back from that because I don't want you to hate me for it later. You deserve to live out your dreams."

"Anna, you *are* my dream," his voice wavered as he moistened his lips and gazed upon Pandora like a unique treasure. "All those college scouts, football- none of that matters without you. We can stay right here and go to Virginia State so we can be closer." Placing his hand in hers, he stroked her cheek with his other finger, "I don't wanna lose you or anything connected to you. I want a family with you someday. Of course, I didn't imagine it being this soon, but it is what it is. We'll figure it out as we go."

An almost electrical feeling came upon Pandora when her eyes connected with the boy she loved. While a baby would most likely ruin any chances of her going to college and getting out of Virginia Beach's cramped town, she clung to Bruce's words like a lifeline. His love carried a road map in her hand the way other girls carried handkerchiefs. Bruce *always* knew the way. His feet were like a compass in her eyes. If he thought they could do it, they could. She wrapped her arms around his neck, fusing her mouth with his and *gosh, was she pretty*, Bruce thought, taking in the texture of her pillow-soft lips.

"I love you," Pandora smiled warmly. "I'll never love anyone the way I love you. Let's do this."

Their young love was so strong and powerful- free in its wildness. It knew nothing of borders, rules, and customs- it was enduring and innocent. But what young love fails to realize when it's young is that the only dependable thing besides death and taxes is change. *Bruce and Pandora had a whole lot of change headed their way*. Helping her up from his lap, they got up and walked hand and hand out of the park.

"So, whose family do we tell first? Mine or yours?" she asked.

Bruce let out a sigh and rubbed the back of his

neck. "Yours. Let's get the crazy side over with first."

Pandora laughed, shaking her head as they began the walk toward her house a few blocks up the road. "I hope my grandmother never finds the shells to her shotgun."

"Bruce Adonis Henry Michael *Steed*!" A woman's stern, but soft voice barked from his front door just as they were passing by.

"Yes, ma'am?" Bruce quickly turned his head to acknowledge his mother glaring at him with folded arms.

"Annabelle Boo-boo," her evil stare faded into a delightful smile when she noticed Pandora beside him, "how are you baby?"

"Hi, Mrs. Steed. I'm fine," Pandora waved, blushing at the ridiculous nickname Bruce's mother had been calling her since elementary school.

"You certainly are. You and that Mannequin have got to be the prettiest little southern belles I ever saw. It's a shame you two waste all of that beauty on those two knuckleheads," her demented glare returned, turning her attention back to her son. "You bring your black behind in this house *right* now and clean up this mess you and Andre made in my kitchen!"

"Sorry mom, I meant to do it after school but I got held up."

"You're getting ready to have my foot held up in your behind," she threatened. "Get in this house! And call Andre over here too."

Bruce turned toward Pandora. "Give me a few minutes, okay?"

"Sure, go ahead," Pandora flagged him. "I'm

gonna go in the house and change anyway. Just come over when you're finished so we can..."

"Yea, sure thing," he kissed her forehead and quickly hopped up his front steps. He tried dodging past his mother, but she gripped his ear and roughly ushered him the rest of the way inside.

"You two stay out of my kitchen *forever*, and I mean it!"

"We were trying to cook breakfast for Quinn and Anna before school, mom. You didn't have to embarrass me like that!"

"From the looks of things, it seems like you both embarrassed yourselves. All this *syrup* and *sugar* everywhere. I'm surprised you didn't put them in a diabetic coma." She closed the door as their voices trailed off.

Pandora giggled and made her way up the block to her own home. Bruce had an amazing family. He had the luxury of growing up with a mother who was open and unassuming, friendly yet careful. His parents had been married for eighteen years and took pride in Bruce and his older sister. They supported every football game, community fish fry, and volunteered at the high school since freshman year. Bruce's sister was a senior in college, and they took care of her two-year-old twins while she was away so she could still get her degree. They were good, wholesome Christians who went to church every week and did what they could to contribute to the good of society.

Her family was another story. Pandora's father, Joseph Senior, was a well-known and respected regional manager for Wells Fargo Bank. Her mother, Sophia, was a seamstress who, after marrying a wealthy Joseph twenty years ago didn't have to work another day of her life so she quit her craft and became a housewife. Pandora's parents were held with high regard and viewed all over town as one of the most humble, caring couples in Virginia. But underneath the surface of their facades lie an ugly reality.

When emotional abuse is shown in movies and television shows, the abuser is often huge and fierce-looking. They never look like the kind-faced person next door. The abuser is never known by his neighbors and doesn't shop at the local stores. He doesn't have friends, doesn't keep a regular job, and is often easy to spot. In real life, however, abusers aren't always that obvious. They might look huge and fierce—but they can also appear gentle and meek - like Joseph Senior.

When Sophia first married Joseph, he prevented her from finishing her education and demanded she quit her job to become a housewife. For as long as Pandora could remember, her father belittled her mother and crushed her self-esteem with his criticism. He put a constant emphasis on how simple-minded she was and how grateful she should be that she got to marry someone like him. Sophia was more like a slave than a wife, and she waited on Joseph 24-7. She often reminded Pandora and her brother, Joseph Jr., to be nice to their father because he had a rough life.

"To hell with his rough life. That doesn't excuse him from making a rough life for the people he claims to love," Pandora fussed at her mother one day after hearing big Joe call Sophia a worthless piece of junk. Pandora couldn't stand his guts, and the feeling was mutual. Joseph hated women and wanted his second child to be a boy. Throughout Sophia's ultrasounds, the technicians and doctors confirmed they would be having another son. As the six-pound, nine-ounce baby came protruding down the birth canal, Joseph's face distorted into sheer disappointment when he saw that *John* turned out to be *Joanna*. Growing up, Big Joe despised his only daughter. He resented her and tried to destroy her confidence the way he did her mother, but it never worked. Every harsh word Joseph spoke, Bruce made Pandora feel the exact opposite. It was through the conflicting relationship between the boy up the street who loved her, and the father who didn't that Pandora learned self-love and emotional intelligence at an early age. She refused to give her father the power to control how she felt about herself. She saw what insecurity and manipulation did to her mother and vowed never to be that weak. Just as Pandora walked up to her porch steps and crept inside the front door, she was met with yelling and screaming coming down the corridor.

"Sophia, have you lost your *mind!* A five hundred dollar prom dress for a *junior* prom?" Joseph roared at his wife, snatching the dress she'd purchased for Pandora and stuffing it back into the boutique's bag.

"Well, you wouldn't let me make her a dress, so we went shopping for a store-bought one, and that's the one she picked out," Sophia defended, following behind her angry husband while he paced the kitchen floor.

"Well take it back and make her pick out

something else. Fifty dollars or less. No woman living in my house without a job is wearing anything that costs five hundred dollars of *my* money. That includes you, too!"

"But it's alright for you to spend *fifteen* hundred dollars on little Joe's football equipment, baseball league, and chess club fees?"

"Yes!" He spun around in a rage, shouting in Sophia's face as beads of spit flew out of his mouth onto the bridge of her nose. "How dare you question me about what I choose to do with my son!"

"I'm not questioning you, I just don't understand why you treat your only daughter this way," Sophia protested in tears.

"Oh no, here goes the guilt trip again," he flung his hands into the air and huffed with an eye roll.

"It's not a guilt trip, Joseph, it's unfair and you know it. That girl has made honor roll since second grade and you've not once told her you were proud of her. You don't come to any of her debates or attend any back to school nights, yet you're always there for little Joe," Sophia shook her head in regret, "that's not okay. You don't support her dreams. To you-" Tired of listening to his wife's accusations, Joseph charged at his wife, backing her into a nearby corner of the kitchen. He forcefully gripped the sides of her face, causing her eyes to widen in fear.

"My mother died five years ago, so stop scolding me and telling me what I'm doing wrong like you're trying to take her place, understood?" he gritted. Sophia shook her head quickly as more tears fell from her eyes.

"Joanna is a girl who will eventually become a woman, which is a dead-end road to nowhere. Women don't have dreams and aspirations; they become stay at home moms who at most, work some form of retail to keep busy. *My son is going to be the next financial advisor, engineer, or president of the United States, so as his father I invest in the things that make him happy. Your* daughter will hopefully follow in your footsteps, find a rich husband and stay out of the way!"

Allowing the front door to close softly, Pandora stepped back in disgust. Devastation fueled her stare as she watched her parents continue their argument through the sheer curtain windowpane on the door. *Don't feed into him, it's not true*, she coached herself. Dropping her school bag on the porch, Pandora rushed down her front steps and hurried around to the side of her house, secluded by trees and bushes. Slamming her back against the brick siding, she closed her eyes and grimaced. Her father was the embodiment of evil. He was rude, uncultured, and just plain disgusting. Although Pandora knew she was strong, she was still human and those horrible words hurt her feelings. *I am somebody. I am not useless. I am worth loving. I'll show him one day.*

Her face trembled involuntarily, but she puckered her lips in an effort to stop the tears. At that point, she wasn't interested in telling her parents that she was expecting. That would only give her father more ammunition to humiliate her. Maybe she could hide it and just deliver without them knowing. *Hell, they never pay attention to me anyway, I'm sure they wouldn't even notice*, she thought, as she began walking back to the front of her house. *Maybe I can-* before she could process the rest of her thought, she felt herself being grabbed from behind. Her arms were forced to their sides by a right arm wrapped around her, holding a knife against her throat. The person's left hand covered her mouth.

"If you scream, I'll *kill* you," the sound of a familiar raspy voice threatened in her ear. Pandora's eyes widened as her body froze in immediate fear. Her mind raced, trying to quickly process what was happening. "You understand me? You scream-you run-*you die.*"

The man's voice was low and deadly. Pandora's heart exploded into her ears when she lowered her eyes to see the knife pressed against her neck. It looked like it could cut through her bones. "Now, you're gonna turn around quickly and walk down those cellar steps behind you."

Pandora felt her chest deflate as her world began spinning on its axis. *Is this some kind of joke?*

Releasing his hand from her mouth, the man motioned for Pandora to turn around. The second she saw a womanly figure in a ski mask opening her neighbor's cellar door, adrenaline flushed through her body as a chilling reality hit her. *No. It's not. This is real.* Quickly and abruptly Pandora started to scream, and the struggle began. The man grabbed her mouth again, but Pandora swung her leg back and kicked him before breaking loose. "Get away from me!" She darted toward her front lawn in an attempt to get into the open so someone could see her.

"You little *cunt!*" the man clenched in pain. Grabbing her by the end of her ponytail, he yanked her down into the grass, and with a venomous pull toward him, he dragged her toward the cellar. Pandora fought, kicked, and struggled, but he was determined.

"Stop it!" she hollered through labored breaths, as her lower body began to disappear into what looked like hell. With her hands, she gripped the edge of the cellar door and held on for dear life. Her head thrashed from side to side like a fire being smothered. There she was, being snatched from the premises of her own backyard. Her home. The safest place on earth. *What an unimaginable intrusion.* With a final violent grip, the man yanked her little body down the remaining steps as hard as he could. Pandora's flesh scraped across the cold cement as her fingernails scratched along the door hinges in a final, feeble protest. The masked accomplice reappeared on the outside and slammed the cellar door. Pandora's heart froze like a brick of ice when she caught a glimpse of her attacker. It was Mr. Perkins, and the woman was his wife, Mrs. Perkins. They were her next-door neighbors and she was now locked in their basement. They were two of the friendliest, loving people Pandora had ever met, but as she caught a glimpse of Mr. Perkins through their struggle, he looked anything but friendly now. He had a wild, emotional look about him. It was tense, like a wire that had been pulled too tight. His once neatly placed gray hair was now straggly as he glared at her through brooding eyes. She didn't understand, *had he lost his mind suddenly? Didn't he know he was hurting her?*

"Mr. Perkins, what are you doing? Stop!" Pandora kicked and cried, wailing her arms. Her pleas were silenced by a hard fist crashing into her mouth, immediately filling it with the metallic taste of blood. Standing over top of her, Mr. Perkins lifted Pandora's head and slammed it into the basement concrete.

"Hold still!" he roared.

Groaning and screaming, Pandora writhed out on the floor clutching her head while he kicked her in her sides with his combat boots. "Please, stop it," she begged faintly. She tried her best to fight him off as agonizing pain pulsated across her body. Mr. Perkins straddled her, wrapped his hands around her neck and squeezed as tight as he could.

"If you scream again, I'll duct tape your mouth shut!" were the last words she heard him say before her air supply and consciousness slipped away. When she came too, she felt fists coming down on her frail body and saw Mr. Perkins staring back at her like a cold-blooded predator. There wasn't the slightest trace of guilt. His lanky old body was massive in comparison to her tiny, hundred-pound frame. By the time he was finished with Pandora, her face was barely recognizable. Her jaw was broken, there were cuts and lacerations all over her lips and a deep slash above her cheek. Her hair was full of dirt, and her mouth was bloody. She babbled and begged with what little fight she had left as her breaths emptied out in slow, shallow rasps. She felt helpless, staring directly into the eyes of a man she thought for sure was going to kill her.

Mrs. Perkins came down the cellar and took off her ski mask. She looked down with those friendly familiar eyes Pandora had known since birth, but her hard stance told her she was anything but a friend now. Kneeling down, she rubbed Pandora's forehead and held her hand with a strong embrace, but it wasn't a warm feeling. It wasn't an act of kindness or love. It felt more like an act of dominance. It said *I am stronger than you are, and don't you ever doubt it. When it comes to you and me; I'm number one.*

At that moment, Pandora signed herself over to them. She couldn't fight anymore. The seventy-year-old pervert kissed her sloppily, leaving a trail of her own bloody drool from her cheeks down to her navel. He ripped her clothes from her body piece by piece. It was like shedding feathers. *Or clipping wings.* His wife knelt down and watched as he began to knead his large fist into her opening. He inserted three and four fingers at a time until Pandora felt something tear. She yelped in pain and started to bleed like a river. Ignoring her cries, he unzipped his pants, held her down and plunged himself into her opening. His flesh ripped through her skin and scissored straight through her organs. It was brutal and violent, and the greatest intrusion on one's person. All that remained unpossessed was her brain. Paralyzed in her own disbelief, Pandora watched through her swollen eyes, cataloging the details of it all. His face, his purpose. *How could he do this to me?* She could feel herself slipping away again, but she forced her body to remain conscious while Mr. Perkins continued his brutal rape, torturously stealing whatever innocence she had left. Focusing on the cellar door above her, she wondered if Bruce had ever made it to her house. They had such a telepathic-like relationship. They finished each other's sentences and often knew how the other was feeling before they came out and said it. Bruce often bragged to others about how he could feel her joy, pain, and fear without her uttering a word. Just before Pandora passed out, she wondered, *Could he feel this?*

Chapter 2

"Nobody can give you freedom. Nobody can give you equality or justice. If you're man enough, you take it."
—Malcolm X

Nine months later

Pandora lay on the floor of the Perkins dungeon curled into a fetal position, bottled up in the horrors that had now become her life. She was wounded and confused, her thoughts as jumbled as a jigsaw puzzle. For nine torturous months, she was raped multiple times a day and brutalized in ways nearly impossible to describe. She was starved and manipulated like an animal. After having her insides ripped and tossed like a salad, the baby she carried with Bruce ceased to exist. Pandora had gone on to become pregnant two more times by Mr. Perkins, but she never made it past the first trimester.

The minute Mrs. Perkins found out about it, she beat them out of her and tossed the dead tissue into the incinerator. Her body had become so mangled and malnourished that it could no longer withstand carrying a child. This was a plus for Mr. Perkins because he didn't have to worry about her getting pregnant anymore. On the days he was too tired to rape her, he would force her to perform sexual acts on him. Everything she'd been taught about modesty, he had robbed her of it. Everything she treasured, he'd stolen it with such pleasure. Pandora peered at the walls through lifeless eyes, hoping her mind could get some rest, but there was never any rest in her brief bouts of sleep. There was never any comfort or solace. Just a hard ground, dirty blankets, and smelly pillows.

Upstairs, the Perkins had an amazing home. Everything looked opulent, from the gleaming wood floors covered in throw rugs, to the sheer curtains billowing like mist on the walls of the floor to ceiling windows. Their furnishings were old, handcrafted workmanship with each area of the room melting into the beauty of the next. There were tall bookcases and fireplaces matted to the walls; it was breathtaking. The basement, however, seemed to be their dirty little secret. It was a total horror show, a dumping ground for scrap lumber, construction debris, gardening tools, *and a sixteen-year-old girl*.

The walls were covered with a combination of efflorescence and peeling paint. The floor was a crumbling concrete covered with layers of dirt and dust. There were cobwebs as thick as nylon stockings at every turn, along with shards of broken glass. The faucets were leaky, the pipes were rusted and damaged, and the stairwell looked like it was made from balsa wood and dental floss. All of the windows were boarded up, except a tiny cracked one in the corner. It was big enough for Pandora to catch glimpses of the outside world but small enough that nobody would have paid any attention to it. You'd never guess by looking at the rest of their home what was in the Perkins' basement, but the line between sanity and madness can be crossed in a single step. The second you opened their cellar door, that's exactly what happened. The Perkins began their journey into Pandora's world years before they actually decided to kidnap her. In fact, they'd practically raised her since she was a month old. Sophia paid them through the years to look after her while she ran errands, but really it was just to get Pandora out of the house because big Joe couldn't stand the sight of her. The Perkins were old enough to be her grandparents and never had any children of their own, so Pandora was a blessing to them. At least, that's what they portrayed. They were a fan favorite of every child in the neighborhood with their beautiful spirits and humble smiles.

Mr. Perkins was the block captain, and Mrs. Perkins always served water ice and pretzels to the kids in the summer. During the months Pandora spent locked in their basement, she learned very quickly that, while many households often had skeletons in their closets, some people kept a closet full of demons. Mr. Perkins loved to talk about his life and purpose. He kept an extensive record of the path he'd taken in life and it was obvious that Pandora would have to hear it all. Through his incessant talking in between Pandora being raped, she learned all about his conviction as a teenager for exposing himself to a small child. She learned about his four marriages and all of the stepchildren he abused. She learned about Mrs. Perkins too. She suffered a miscarriage twenty-five years ago at five months pregnant and fed their dead baby's remains to her pet snake with a smile. She longed for a child after that, and Mr. Perkins longed for a new toy to play with. They always overheard Sophia and Joseph's constant bickering through the walls about how much Joseph hated his daughter, so they decided Pandora would be the one they took.

Shortly after Sophia had settled her new bundle of joy into her home, the Perkins began positioning themselves to be in the right place at the right time. Mr. Perkins offered to rake leaves and repair the roof so he could survey the area of her home and look for any windows he could creep through. Over the years, they manipulated their way into her house in order to find out the location of each bedroom, and where Pandora slept. They knew what time she left and returned from school as well. Soon, they were able to take Pandora off her mother's hands by allowing her to come to their house after school. Through having Pandora in their home, they earned her trust, learned her temperament, and all the things that made her vulnerable. *And then they waited*...Patiently. They wanted to be certain that when they made their move, it would be a permanent one, and any chances of them being looked at as possible suspects were null and void. In the blink of an eye, Pandora had gone from a straight-A student with a comfortable life, to starving hunger, fatigue, and thirst. She felt a nakedness that bared her to the bones.

Two days after they stole Pandora from her yard, Mrs. Perkins announced, "I am your mother, and he's your new husband." Pandora raised an eyebrow, and the word *crazy* rolled around her head.

Every day she experienced embarrassment and shame so deep, she felt worthless. There was always pain and burning, intruding hands, leary dark eyes, and a heartbreaking yearning to go home. From concentration camps to war experiences, history proves that people can survive unspeakable traumas, yet there is no neat and tidy explanation as to how they do it. Core elements keep hope alive in some way; thinking about the future, and having something to occupy your mind to prevent dwelling on reality. Some of the defense mechanisms that are occasioned by trauma often help victims through horrific experiences. Memories of Quinn's innocent smile and Eden's obnoxious laughter; those were the moments Pandora locked inside of her brain after she had been captured. She remembered giggling through her childhood with them, eating snacks and doing homework at each other's houses. In school, Quinn and Pandora sat and ate together every day. She remembered Quinn's bougie attitude, sneering at her lunch tray in disgust when the lunch lady made her food touch on the plate. Pandora once learned that when someone dies, the very first thing you forget is the sound of their voice. The thought of her not remembering Bruce and his deep baritone voice terrified her, so she began to reminisce on the little things they'd said to one another each day.

"Hey baby, you up?" She remembered his untimely <u>three a.m.</u> phone calls. She used to hate when he woke her up in the middle of the night, but she would have given anything to hear his voice again. Those were the memories Pandora had clung too, now that everything was gone.

She survived each day by listening to the outside world from the small window. It was full of life and familiar voices, and she'd often imagine she was a part of it. The day Pandora was kidnapped she could hear Bruce banging on her front door, frantically asking her parents where she was. They called her cell phone but it was left in her school bag on the front porch. A passerby walking a dog knocked on her door. He said he heard a young female screaming near her house, but when he doubled back with his dog, he didn't see anyone. That was all it took. By 10:16 pm, the police arrived, and by 10:20, news had spread so quickly, the entire neighborhood arrived; *including the Perkins*.

By 10:30 pm, there was panic, chaos, and pandemonium all throughout Pandora's house. Detectives found traces of her ponytail extensions and blood left behind in the grass that Mrs. Perkins failed to clean up. It was announced that after putting up a struggle, Pandora had been kidnapped. The police questioned her parents like criminals, asking the same things over and over in different ways to make sure their stories weren't tainted. Pandora could even hear them interrogating her friends and boyfriend.

"What kind of girl is Joanna? Is she promiscuous? How is she in school? Has she ever experimented with drugs? Were you jealous of her?" they asked Quinn and Eden. "How long have you guys dated? Was she cheating on you? Did you have her killed?" they glared at Bruce.

"If you don't leave these *got* damn kids alone!" Pandora could hear Miss Ruby bursting into outrage at the authorities, "Anna is a *good* girl with *good* grades. Stop trying to criminalize her just to have something negative to say to the media. Find the actual criminal that took her!"

By midnight, volunteers were gathered in small groups led by the Perkins as they canvassed the neighborhood. They knocked on doors and talked to people in other neighborhoods, explaining what happened. Joseph Senior pretended to be concerned, but in his mind, he figured Pandora had run off somewhere and was probably doing all of this for attention. Sophia was terrified and filled with so much guilt that she was incoherent. Her sister offered her a sedative, but she declined. She heard the front door close in the midst of her arguing with her husband that afternoon, and she knew Pandora heard them.

Had she finally taken enough emotional abuse from her father and run away from home? Sophia felt like she'd failed as a mother and wished she would have left her obnoxious husband years ago before things had gotten this bad. Whatever had happened to Pandora, Sophia felt responsible for it. Within a week's time, alerts had gone out to the media, and information about Pandora's abduction started to crawl across the bottom of television screens. The radio stations started relaying information, and by the next month, the national media was camped outside of her backyard. Volunteers had multiplied into the thousands, searching high and low for her. Websites had her picture plastered all over them, and a $250,000 reward was offered for information that led to her being rescued.

Over the next few months, the search expanded beyond Virginia and swelled to thousands of people across the

USA. There were volunteers with bloodhounds, and churches who contributed flashlights, coffee, food, and batteries. There were helicopters searching the mountains, and milk cartons with her face on it. It seemed the world had searched everywhere, *except fifty feet away in the house next door.* After the long searches had ended for the night, Mr. Perkins would come down into his cellar, smiling proud at what he had captured and hid from the world. Mr. Perkins wasn't clinically psychotic or delusional. He was a manipulative, narcissistic pedophile. *He was just an evil man.*

After six months of searching, Pandora listened intently as the town had given up and mourned her as if she were dead. There was no reason for them to believe she was alive, and no reason for anyone to believe she was ever coming home. Pandora watched her mother set up a memorial on her front steps so people could come by and pay their respects. After that, the mourning stopped and the world went on. The seasons changed without her, the holidays came and left, and her parents seem to live life as if Pandora never existed. The only people who refused to give up hope were Bruce, Quinn, Andre, Miss Ruby, and Eden.

The love Bruce had for Pandora could be felt a million miles away. His heart was broken beyond repair, and it began to affect his future. He barely went to school and his poor attendance caused him to be cut from his football team. Almost every day, Pandora watched him play hooky just to come and sit at her memorial and talk to her as if she were right there. If he'd only turned around and looked through the small window to the left, he would've seen that she *was*. Some days, Pandora considered screaming for help, but she knew it would be useless. Her body didn't have the energy to give off the kind of scream that was needed to be heard from a basement cellar, and even if someone did hear her, the Perkins would've killed her before anyone realized where the screaming came from.

One day, Pandora watched Miss Ruby as she sat on Pandora's front porch hugging a depressed Quinn and consoling an angry Eden who'd been asking a million and one questions as to why Pandora hadn't been found yet.

"Mom, why does God allow things like this to happen?" Eden asked through her tears. "Why does evil like this exist in the world? You always said we serve the God of a *turnaround* and *second chances*," she mocked. "Why doesn't he turn this evil into something good and bring Anna back?" Ruby pulled Eden into her embrace and wiped away her tears.

"God *is able* to make some good come from evil. But even He, in all his splendor, won't make the evil go away. Humans are given free will. He won't control them. There is wickedness in this world and choices to make. When you're faced with good and evil you have to make a *choice*. You can *choose* to be swallowed up by the evil, or you can embrace the good." Pandora's own tears trickled from her frail cheeks as Ruby's words seemed to hang in the air between them. *You can choose to be swallowed up by the evil, or you can embrace the good.*

That day, a flame lit inside of her. A fierce determination that no matter what, she was going to *survive.* Eventually, Pandora grew a shell, the beginning of her defense mechanism. She became a hard-boiled egg, nodded her head, did everything she was asked and didn't bother to argue. *Whatever it took to live.* She gave up wallowing in her self-pity and learned to be grateful for the good. A pure rush of gratitude overtook Pandora anytime she could sleep with the realization that she would survive another day. She learned to be grateful for small victories like food, water, and a few hours of the day when she wasn't being raped. She learned the ability to slip into a quiet, painless place, a state of pure survival where she could shut the world out and rest. She often thought of Mr. and Mrs. Perkin's salt and pepper hair and the fact that they had to be somewhere in their seventies, which meant she would outlive them. *It might be 20, maybe 30 years from now, but one day they're going to die. And when they do, I will be free.*

That evening, as the daylight began to come to an end, the town gathered together in front of Pandora's home in preparation for a final memorial service. Senior year was set to begin tomorrow, and Salem High School prepared a scholarship event in Pandora's honor. Since she was so involved in extracurricular activities and had dreams of going to college, her parents donated all of the money raised to aid in her rescue to her high school. Salem High created, "The Joanna Scholarship" for an active student who served on the student council or debate team that couldn't afford a collegiate education. The first honoree that would receive the scholarship was Rosemarie

Winters. Pandora peered through the window of the cellar with her arms folded. She remembered Rosemarie from Junior High after she exposed her breasts to Bruce in the cafeteria.

"The nerve of them to send a *whore* to college in my honor," she rolled her eyes in disgust.

As the mayor walked onto her porch to begin the service, a wavering smile formed on Pandora's pale face. She looked around at all of her classmates she had grown up with, and they all appeared to have aged so wonderfully since junior year. She felt like a hundred years old compared to everyone, but she was still happy for them. She saw Bobby Johnson and Phillip Pierce, the two class clowns who swore they were dropping out last year to audition for a rock band. Pandora's disappearance straightened them out and gave them a new appreciation for life and education. Even though they didn't have plans of going to college, they vowed to finish high school in her name.

Pandora's eyes surveyed the crowd. Her eyes lit up when she saw Julia Broach, Leslie Peters, and Isaiah Thomas taking their seats. They were her friends from the debate team, and she was in awe of how much more mature they looked. Her heart skipped a beat when she saw Eden and Miss Ruby. Eden had grown a few inches taller and finally began filling out into her curves. Almost overnight, she seemed to have gone from a shy faced little girl to a beautiful teenager. She rested against her mother, who leaned on a nearby light pole, keeping an arm securely wrapped around Eden's waist.

Pandora loved their relationship. It was the most beautiful example of a mother-daughter bond that she'd ever seen. Pandora's smile grew wider when she saw Andre consoling Quinn near the side of her house. Quinn had an irritated look about her. She had grown annoyed with these pointless memorial services and wasn't interested in attending another one. She was sick of listening to empty prayers and rest in peace poems. Quinn wanted her best friend back, and she still had hope that God would help them find her. Andre stood in front of Quinn, wiping her tears away with his stubby fingers. The intense passion those two felt for each other was the reason Pandora still believed in fairy tales. Their love was inexplicable. Even though Andre was the son of a preacher, he was rough, tough, and known to have a terrible temper at times. It made him a force to be reckoned with on the football field, but whenever Quinn was in his presence, his demeanor shifted like magic. Quinn had the palest gray eyes Pandora had ever seen on a human being. They were frozen with a welcome home warmth to them. She watched Andre lose himself in them every time Quinn stared at him. They were perfect for one another. Finally, Pandora saw Bruce and her stomach filled with butterflies and twisted into knots. He went away to a live-in camp over the summer, so Pandora hadn't seen him sitting by her memorial since the end of last school year. Bruce looked as if puberty had struck him again. He had grown taller and more athletically defined. He grew facial hair and had gotten a few tattoos. Pandora bit her lip and blushed as she watched him slap fives with Andre and gently hug Quinn while they reunited, quietly conversing amongst themselves. Although Bruce smiled and laughed, Pandora could still see the pain etched into his eyes. Pain that would forever be embedded into his DNA. Bruce's love for Pandora was so raw. To be loved like that at such a young age was a gift from God. Being wrapped in Bruce's arms held an inexpressible warmth, peace, and bliss. Every heart in this world yearns for only two common things, *love, and God.* Through Bruce, Pandora believed that Love was the other name of God, the form in which human beings can attain. They *had* it, and life *stole* it from them.

Pandora's precious moments were cut short by the cellar door wildly swinging open, hitting the back of the wall. Mr. Perkins made his way down the noisy steps, drunk and disheveled, using both hands to hang on to the wall. "Good evening, Anna," his voice slurred, "It's a beautiful evening outside." Pandora turned away from the window, positioning herself into a corner. This was the first time she had ever seen Mr. Perkins drunk. He always claimed to be a prophet of God, using religion to justify all of his sick actions. She wondered what his excuse would be for being intoxicated.

"Hello," her timid voice blurted out. Pressing her elbows to the sides, Pandora tried to make her body as small as possible in hopes that he would go back upstairs and leave her alone.

"I missed you, sweetheart, did you miss me?" With a Grinch-like smile, Mr. Perkins staggered over to Pandora to caress her cheek, but stumbled over his own two feet and fell to the ground.

"Jesus Christ, I can't go to your memorial like this," he said, using the wall to help him to his feet, drooling along the way. "I went out to eat with one of my old students. I ordered seltzer water, but they must've pranked me and laced it with alcohol or something because I think I'm drunk. That *idiot*. God will condemn him to hell for poisoning a prophet."

Right. Apparently, God could command him to move mountains, part the seven seas, and call down fire from heaven but he couldn't help him realize he was drinking liquor instead of seltzer water, Pandora thought.

"I'm sorry," she replied, "how about you go lie down and take a nap." Mr. Perkins laughed out loud, his voice low and guttural.

"I can't *lie down* silly, I have to go to your memorial and put on a show for the neighborhood. Why don't *you* lie down and open your legs so I can relieve myself before I go."

Pandora's body felt like it was rooted in place. She never got used to being violated against her will. It seemed to be more frightening each time. Pandora stared up at him through damp, overly bright eyes, refusing to move, hoping he would be too drunk to notice.

"What are you doing? I said get down on the floor!" he fussed. Gripping her by her elbow, Mr. Perkins jerked Pandora forward, slammed her into the ground, and raped her. Little did he know this time would prove to be his *last*.

After finishing, he collapsed on the side of her in a drunken stupor. Pandora kept her eyes squeezed shut the entire time, counting back from 100 to take her mind off of what was going on. When she realized it was over she slowly opened her eyes, trembling in fear. She quickly slid away from him and stood up to adjust her dirty nightgown. She felt vile and disgusting as if taking a hundred showers couldn't rid her of his stench. She could hear Mrs. Perkins exiting the house, motioning for Quinn to come give her a hug and talk to her. *That's* when Pandora realized it. *Mr. Perkins* was passed out, and *Mrs. Perkins* was outside, which meant a smooth escape was right in her grasp.

Her heart began to race as she walked to the bottom of the steps and saw the open cellar door. *Can I make it? What if Mrs. Perkins gets back into the house before I can get out? She'd kill me. What if the front door is bolted shut? Suppose some kind of alarm goes off?* Her mind went into overdrive, making her dizzy and sick with uncertainty and fear. Pandora rushed to peer out the window and saw Quinn motioning Mrs. Perkins further away from her house to come say hello to her mother. It was almost as if Quinn was purposely creating a diversion in Pandora's favor.

From the moment Pandora had been captured, she was a pawn in the Perkins' hands. Naked. Hurting. Terrified. No power. No dignity. No freedom over her body, what she drank, what she ate. Today, she decided she was going to take it back *or die trying*. Without thinking it over any further, she rushed up the creeping basement stairs, carefully checking one last time to make sure the noise didn't awaken Mr. Perkins. When she reached the top and walked out of the cellar door, it was like falling over a waterfall. She stared at the front door with wide eyes, holding in the urge to scream. *This was it.* Without any more hesitation, Pandora sprinted like an Olympic gold medalist toward the Perkins' front door. Her knees shook, and her legs nearly gave away but she kept running. She opened the front door and began running toward her freedom. She looked back at her prison as it receded further and further into the distance. *She was doing it.* She made a vow to herself, and it had come to pass. *She had broken free.* At that moment it was as if she too, knew why the caged bird sings. As the evening air hit her body, she almost fainted. She hadn't seen the light of day in over nine months. Pandora raced down the Perkins' lawn, putting herself into the view of the crowd at her memorial service. Uncontrollable tears flooded from her eyes, tainting her vision, but she didn't care. *"Help me!"* She screamed until her tonsils burned.

The audience turned toward her sound and she could hear them burst into bouts of loud shrills and gasps. The noise caused Bruce's eyes to break away from the mayor's speech. Just as he turned, Pandora caught his view. His eyes flicked straight and without preamble, into a direct gaze with hers. Time suddenly felt like it was moving in slow motion. Bruce tried to yell, but no words could come out of his mouth. He began to run, but his legs felt like hundred-pound weights holding him back. "Anna!" he yelled in a panic.

The memorial service went into an emotional uproar as people began racing toward her. Some of them stared in absolute shock like Pandora was a ghost. The dead was alive! Eden screamed, Quinn's heart skipped beats, Sophia fainted on the grass, and Miss Ruby seemed to stop breathing. For a moment, Pandora's world seemed to absolutely stop. She stared at the crowd and the crowd stared back at her. Suddenly, *n*ine months of fear and pain melted with what remained of the sun. She felt a sweet assurance. *Freedom...At. Last.*

Chapter 3

Forever Mine

Virginia State University- Sophomore year.

Pandora and Quinn sat in the stands of the Virginia State University football field, giggling at the tacky cheerleaders and doing homework while they waited for the football team to finish practicing.

"This has been the worst semester *ever*," Pandora fussed, her gaze bounced from place to place on her laptop screen.

"Tell me about it," Quinn huffed, looking through her child development notes, "Have you ever had Dr. Brookstone for child development?

"I haven't, but I know people who have. I hear she's cutthroat with her exams."

"*Oh my g*oodness, she is ridiculous. Her classes make me so discombobulated. Our midterm is this Friday and although I've studied for weeks there's still so much more material to cover."

"You'll do just fine Miss 4.0," Pandora mocked, playful jealousy laced her voice. *"Meanwhile*, I have Dr. Webber for accounting. My life has been formulas and statistics for the last week and a half."

"Ew," Quinn winced in disgust, "Math makes my skin itch. For someone who had no interest in college, you sure chose one heck of a major."

"I didn't choose it. Miss Ruby chose it *for* me. If I had it my way, I would have been a hospitality major," Pandora muttered. Quinn burst into laughter.

"Hospitality? Pandora, *what* part of you is hospitable?"

"Excuse me? I consider myself to be *very* hospitable," she folded her arms, looking at Quinn in offense, "I would've fit beautifully in a hotel management position."

"Oh please. I can see it now," Quinn grabbed her cellphone, putting it up to her ear. "*Good Morning sir, this is Anna from reservations. I see that you requested a king-sized, pool-view room on a high floor nowhere near an elevator. Would you like it to face a three-legged flying unicorn that poops gold as well?*" she laughed.

"*Whatever*," Pandora nudged Quinn, amused.

"Now, don't get me wrong, I think you have a gift of serving others, but you need to do it in a field suitable for a headstrong, argumentative, determined woman. Customer service is *not* it."

"Headstrong?" Pandora gasped, clutching her chest, "Me?" They both simultaneously broke into laughter. Suddenly, a cheerleader on the field attempted to jump out of a human pyramid and landed flat on her face. Quinn and Pandora laughed harder, causing some of the cheerleaders to look into the stands and roll their eyes.

"What a mess. They're not even paying attention to what they're doing,"

"That's because they're too busy trying to be cute for the guys," Pandora replied.

"Whose bright idea was it to have all of these horny girls share a practice with a bunch of football players?"

"I bet it was Miss Boyd. You know they appointed her as the new cheer coach after Boe left," Pandora confirmed, reaching into her school bag to grab her textbook.

"Miss Boyd?" Quinn jerked her head back, "how did she manage to cut in front of all those people who were next in line for coach? That's not fair."

"Of course it isn't, but when you're screwing the Dean of Students, you can pretty much do what you want," Pandora raised an eyebrow. Quinn's bottom jaw nearly hit the ground.

"Shut the front door! Are you serious?"

"Serious as a heart attack, honey. I swear you live under a rock. This has been floating around campus since last year after Miss Boyd got caught leaving his house at 3 am."

"Oh my. How *awful*," Quinn shook her head remorsefully, "The Dean's wife is such a nice lady too."

"She must not have been handling business correctly. It happens."

"It's *still* a shame."

"Well from the looks of things, *you're* not handling your business correctly, either," Pandora snorted, watching Andre being dragged into a tackle, "Your man is getting mangled out there." Quinn looked up at Andre with an incredulous stare and slammed her eyes shut after watching him being tossed onto the ground and pounced on by four other players.

"Poor thing. That's because they have that stupid running back playing the substitute. Where in the world is Bruce?

He hasn't been out here to play his position all practice. I thought I saw him on the field earlier," Quinn's eyes searched the lower sidelines. The sound of Bruce's name caused Pandora's entire demeanor to shift.

"Why would I know? *Or* care?" Reverting her attention back to her notebook, Pandora glared at it.

Quinn cut an eye at her, sensing Pandora's sudden onset of anger.

"You wouldn't…" Quinn hesitated, "I'm sorry." She turned her head toward the cheerleaders and left it alone. After a long silence, it felt like a huge elephant filled the atmosphere and took up the entire football field. Bruce was a sore spot for Pandora, and likewise- Pandora was a sore spot for Bruce. Their failed love was a huge issue through the years that everyone was aware of but dared not discuss with either of them. As concerned as Quinn was, she wouldn't have touched it with a ten-foot pole. After breaking out of the Perkins' dungeon two years ago, Pandora's life made a dramatic shift.

The Perkins' were arrested and immediately charged with rape, abduction of a minor and aggravated sexual battery. As they rotted in prison awaiting a trial, Pandora couldn't bear to live in her neighborhood another second. She could no longer stomach the sight of her weak mother or deal with the blatant feminine ignorance of her father. She grew tired of pretending to be one big happy family and fed up with living a lie. She also couldn't bear to live next door to a house that had been her prison for almost a year. Pandora hated going to school as well because everyone treated her as if she were some sort of freak show. There were whispers from teachers as she walked her high school halls, and pedestrians stopping to take pictures of her as she walked home from school. Others kept their distance. Finally, she moved in with Miss Ruby and Eden.

"Anna, there hasn't yet been a word created by man to describe what these people have done to you and how wickedly evil they are! They've stolen a piece of your life that you'll never get back." Ruby took Pandora's bags and knelt down as she bored into her eyes, *"However, the best punishment you can give them is to be happy and move forward with your life. While this trial will most likely deliver a harsh sentence for them, you may never feel like justice has been served or restitution has been granted. But I don't want you to worry about that because at the end of it all, God is our ultimate judge. He has the final say and he will restore every second of pain and loss that you've suffered. I promise."* Pandora clung to Miss Ruby's words and vowed to obey.

Two months later, the Perkins went to trial and Pandora took the stand. The world watched on national television, a tormented young girl as she spoke from her heart, emptying all of the pain, shame, fear, and embarrassment she'd suffered at the hands of the Perkins'. She described every rape, every forced pregnancy, abortion, and weeks gone by without food. By the time she finished, there wasn't a dry eye in the courtroom. Unfortunately, after the workings of a good defense attorney who managed to prove that the Perkins were both temporarily insane, they were acquitted of all charges and given six years of psychiatric custody. After which, they would be let back into society. When the verdict was read, the state of

Virginia went into a *riot.* Pandora sat in the courtroom with an empty gaze, completely numb. She watched Mr. Perkin's sadistic grin eyeing her from his seat while he mouthed the words, *"See you soon."*

Miss Ruby watched Pandora's attitude go downhill that year. Grief, bad news, and disappointment caused her to become downtrodden. The once happy child that Ruby knew was now permanently moody, aggressive, and temperamental. She hated *all* men, beginning with her father. She grew an independent chip on her shoulder and acted as if she didn't need anyone to help her. Bruce tried his best to be there for her but she acted as if she hated him too. Pandora would ignore his phone calls, rip up his love notes, and dodge him in school. Finally, she told Bruce she wasn't ready to be back into a relationship, and she dumped him. Bruce was heartbroken. He didn't understand why Pandora kept pushing him away but he refused to give up. He put his manhood and ego on the line repeatedly, even asking her to the senior prom. Pandora denied his request, but wickedly, she made sure to take one of his friends from the football team instead. After seeing her with his teammate, Bruce finally gave up. He'd lost his football scholarship to every D1 university, *and* his dignity all in the name of a love that made a *fool* out of him.

The hatred Pandora felt for Bruce became mutual and neither of them could stand the sight of the other. After high school, they both ended up at Virginia State and pretended the other never existed. Bruce majored in criminal justice and had become a star running back for the football team. He also became a whore. He had women at his disposal and used them for his sexual advantage. After sleeping around, he made a name for himself and had nearly every girl on campus single *and* dating wanting to be in his bed. Pandora was a Business Management major and president of the Virginia State debate team. Her dark days of captivity had played a permanent part in shaping her, at times *wrenching* her into the heartless human being she had become. It was perfect for the debate team. Pandora was deliberate, beautiful, and afraid of nothing. She walked with a vengeance and wasn't interested in relationships, casual dating, or sex. There were plenty of guys who flirted and attempted to get to know her but she treated them as if they were gum under her shoe. Ruby and her best friends were her only soft spots in life, and she was content with that. Pandora knew deep down that there would eventually be a psychological price to pay for her cold emotions, but she was determined to control her life as best as she could until it happened. Throwing the rest of her things into her bag, Pandora stood up and snatched her purse.

"I should get going, I have a debate meeting in a few minutes." Quinn placed her things in her bag and stood up with her.

"Okay, well I'm gonna head to Andre's room and wait up for him, so walk with me before you go," Quinn requested sweetly.

"Fine," Pandora muttered with an attitude. They both walked down the bleachers and made their way to the boy's dormitory in silence. Quinn knew Pandora didn't have any kind of debate practice. She was only trying to get away from the uncomfortable energy that Bruce's name had brought on.

"I love you," Quinn gently bit her lip, breaking through the silence. She looked up at Pandora with puppy dog eyes. Pandora cut her eyes at Quinn and pressed her lips into a slight grimace. She couldn't stay agitated with her if her life depended on it. She giggled at Quinn's innocent expression and put an arm around her.

"You make me *sick,*" Pandora replied as they both shared a laugh.

"You wanna hang out with me until Andre gets back? I'm sure it'll be pretty lonely at your imaginary debate meeting." Quinn pulled out her keys and unlocked Andre's door.

"I'll hang out for a few minutes, but then I have to meet Clarissa for din-" They both stopped dead in their tracks when Andre's door swung open and they were met with Pandora's debate teammate Clarissa, swallowing Bruce's manhood like her life depended on it while Bruce leaned against the dresser, shirtless.

"Ooh," Quinn gasped. She quickly turned around, tripping over her own feet to get out of the room. Pandora, on the other hand, decided to stay awhile.

"*Ooh* it's hot in here," she raised an eyebrow, leaning against the door with a smirk. Bruce opened his eyes and snapped his head in Pandora's direction. He tore away from the wall and almost choked Clarissa to death with his erection.

"Shoot!" He yelped, snatching Clarissa's head off of him as he tried to reach for a towel. Clarissa gagged and choked, turning toward the dorm room door. The minute she regained control of her vocal cords, she squealed in embarrassment, nearly jumping out of her skin. "Close the door, Anna, what the hell!" Bruce hollered. Pandora watched with a Grinch-like smirk, enjoying seeing them scuffle around for their clothes.

"Why? Every girl on campus has been in your bed. No need for discretion *now*," she teased and walked out, making sure to leave the door wide open for everyone's viewing pleasure. Quinn stood out in the hallway looking like she had just seen a ghost.

"Isn't that Jason's *girlfriend*?"

"It sure is," Pandora shook her head in disgust, "That's so lo-" Before she could finish her sentence, a strong hand gripped her arm and yanked her. Pandora's entire body flew out of Quinn's reach.

"We need to talk," Bruce demanded with a demented glare, pulling Pandora with one arm and securing his towel with the other.

"Excuse me, you can take your *filthy* hands off of me after you just got finished touching that so-called *virgin*," Pandora fussed, trying to jerk her way out of his touch. Clarissa hurried out of Bruce's room, but not before rolling her eyes at Pandora's comment. She wanted to curse her out but she knew better of it. Quinn stood in the distance, frozen in fear. This was the first time in two years that Bruce and Pandora had interacted with each other, and she wasn't sure what to make of the situation. Bruce snatched Pandora into his bedroom and slammed the door.

"Are you serious, leaving my door wide open like that?" He yelled in her face. "That was my teammate's girlfriend, you could've gotten me into a heap of trouble!"

"*I* could have gotten you into trouble?" Pandora jerked her head back, looking at Bruce like he was crazy, "*I* didn't do anything. That's on *you* for being dirty and grimy to your friends!"

"How about you mind your business!"

"Well that's hard to do seeing as you've made your vainglorious sex life everybody's business," she pursed her lips. Bruce glared back at her angrily before stepping back and pointing toward the door.

"Get the hell out of my room. And next time, k*nock*."

"It's not just *your* room, it's Andre's, too, and if I don't feel like knocking, *I won't*!" she hissed back. Her mind, although filled with rage, couldn't help but notice that Bruce was standing half-naked in front of her. Pandora was shocked that a thought like that even registered in her mind. Men didn't seem to catch her attention since senior year of high school.

Bruce's skin was an exotic mahogany and if she remembered correctly, it was coffee ground smooth. He stood in front of her, barrel-chested and bow-legged with a frame so defined, it demanded your attention whether you liked it or not. Without warning, old feelings that Pandora swore she'd burned alive began to resurface. She remembered the pure rush of energy between them that was so intense, it felt like the galaxies collided every time they connected. She remembered his hands were like branding irons that scorched his identity into her heart. She remembered the pads of his fingertips, they were like printing blocks used to tap permanent messages of meaning into her body. The show of vulnerability had cut right through Pandora and it made her extremely uncomfortable that she couldn't control it. She tried to swallow past the lump growing in her throat but it was becoming increasingly difficult. Bruce's mischievous brown eyes studied her, and a devious smile tilted his lips. He could see Pandora's demeanor and was enjoying her discomfort.

Get it together, her mind screamed, forcing her to look in a safer direction.

"Do you need help finding the door, sweetheart?" He grinned, raising a midnight black eyebrow, "Because I can assure you it's not under my towel." Pandora felt a sudden fire creep into her cheeks. She wasn't amused and she was even less pleased by the fact that she was losing her composure.

"I know where the *door* is," she retorted, getting her mind together. Another smile snaked across Bruce's face. This annoyed her.

"Good seeing you, Anna. Too bad we ran into each other on terms like this. I hear you're quite the fire on campus. I'm proud of you."

"And I hear you're quite the man-whore, and your GPA is subpar. I'm sure your dead father is smiling down from heaven," she declared angrily. Bruce's eyeballs nearly bulged out of his sockets at her comment. A stray bullet killed his father last year and Bruce had been suffering in silence. He knew his coping mechanisms and the different things he'd been doing weren't the greatest, but no one ever had the guts to throw it in his face before. Pandora could feel the venom seeping through his veins, and finally, she felt like she had regained control over the situation. She turned to walk out of his room but he grabbed her and pushed her back against the door.

"You need to keep my father's name out of your mouth," he pointed in her face, "and for your information, I'm on the verge of getting a 3.0 this semester."

"*Oh please*, if you were Pinocchio your nose would be twenty miles long right now."

"Whatever," Bruce stepped back. If she were a man he would've knocked her teeth loose. "I don't have anything to prove to you. You're *nothing* to me."

"Oh, good!" she perked up her posture, "then stop *lying* to me. Lie to your family and your hoes. They love you. *I don't*." A tidal wave of rage overtook Bruce. He could feel his blood boiling beneath his skin.

"You say *one* more thing in reference to my family *or my father,* and I'll-"

"You'll do *what*, Bruce? You'll grow up and get it together? Because right now you're nothing but a trifling, scumbag whore on a scholarship. You're a waste of tax dollars and a disappointment to your mother and whoever else is left to pick up the pieces of raising you!" She shouted at the top of her lungs.

"And you're a big disappointment to the *entire world*!" Bruce burst into a fit of rage. "I'm so happy you got raped! Why don't you go back to that dungeon and rot, you evil wench!" As soon as the words left his mouth, he regretted them. Pandora raised her eyebrows and gave Bruce a stare that bordered pure menace. He'd seen that look before in the blank stares of sociopaths and psychotic killers on Law and Order. It instantly made him nervous. Immediately, tears filled Pandora's eyes. She didn't have a comeback after that. *He won.* His harsh words had cut to the white meat. Instantly, she lost track of the person she'd fought so hard to become over the last two years. At that moment she felt powerless, perplexed, useless, and weak. Her hand began to tremble as she reached behind her for the doorknob. "Wait, I'm sorry," Bruce's voice shook, quickly grabbing her hand from the door. Pandora snatched her hand away and tried to reach for the handle again.

"Stay away from me," she tried to scream, but embarrassment clawed itself around her vocal cords and held on tight so it was more like a squeal. Bruce snatched her into his arms like a rag doll and held on for dear life as Pandora fought to get out of his grasp. The feel of having her wrapped in his possession forced a small tear down his own cheek. He didn't mean those harsh words. It was never Bruce's intention to grow hatred in his heart for her, period. Pandora was his everything. He remembered the first day he fell in love with her. First, it was her smile. Then, it was her dimples. He could never really pinpoint one specific quality, but he knew he wanted her. *All of her.* Forever. When he lost her, his only motive in life was to get her back. Over the years, his emotions for Pandora were so sensitively wrapped up in every bad thing that had happened to her that it made him completely restless. All the time. His heart uncontrollably beat for her. He found himself daydreaming and distant from reality. His mind swayed like a tree in a storm. Bruce tried forcing himself to hate Pandora, but true love didn't work like that, so he ran from himself. Over the years, he found himself subconsciously searching for Pandora in anything that looked and smelled like a woman, but he was unsuccessful. As he held her in his arms, his mind raced a mile a minute. It felt so surreal, he wondered, *Did my heart ever love until now?*

"Stop it," he ordered, refusing to let her go.

"Bruce, let me *go!*" Pandora screamed in a vengeful, unforgiving voice.

"I'm sorry!" He shouted back.

"Go to he-"

"*I love you*," his voice shook, interrupting her. Those words caused Pandora to become frozen stiff. Her eyes locked onto his. "I need you…I love you…*Please* come back to me," he pleaded, "tell me you love me back." Pandora glared at Bruce. She struggled to hold on to her sanity, but she felt herself slipping away and she *knew* he could see it. Bruce reached down to kiss her, and at that moment she realized there was nothing else in the world that she wanted. Finally, Pandora did something she refused to do for a very long time. *She let go.*

When Bruce's lips met hers, it wasn't a sweet or gentle kiss. It was a fiercely hungry one that stole her breath away. Bruce touched all over Pandora as if he were erasing her outer shell, forcing her to reveal her inner self. Brick by brick her wall came tumbling down. She tried coaching her mind to run from him, but her body refused. Without warning, she broke free from his kiss, slammed herself into his chest and broke down into tears. Her emotions were raw and unprocessed as her sobs tore through her muscles. *Over and Over. In and Out.* Bruce could feel her heart yanking in and out of her chest, pulling back in like a yo-yo. There was a rawness to it, as if her pain was still an open wound. Pandora felt like a hollow shell, like her life was crumbling in his arms. He held on to her and caressed her back like he had carved a sculpture and was now feeling its finish, smoothing out any rough areas.

"I love you," she looked up at Bruce, not bothering to wipe the evidence of heartache from her face, "No matter how much I have pushed you away, *I love you*."

"Why did you do this to us?"

"Because I didn't feel like a person anymore after what happened. I felt filthy and disgusting. After everyone knew what had been done to me, why would *anyone* want me back? Why would anyone still love me? Who would ever want to talk to me or be my friend?" She squeezed her eyes as if she were being forced to relive the pain a second time. "I felt like a beautiful vase that was accidentally knocked off the window sill. No, it wasn't the vase's fault, but it was still thrown to the floor and shattered. It's still broken. It's still worthless, and you don't want it anymore so you sweep it up and throw it away."

"But *I* wanted you. I *still* want you," Bruce replied, "I would never reject you, no matter what anyone has done to you."

Pandora wrapped her arms around Bruce's neck, allowing him to feel down her frame. He took in the texture of her skin, and all the hills and valleys that made up the landscape of who she was.

"Be mine, again. *Forever* this time," he requested.

"I just…I can't take picturing the things you've done to all these girls on campus. They talk about it all the time and it's like I can see it in my head. I just wish I could go back to when…when I never let you go, and I could pretend like it's only *ever* been me."

Bruce dropped to his knees in front of her, fully aware that he was begging but not having the will to care.

"It *has* only ever been you. In every way that matters. The things that happened when we were apart only means something if we let it mean something."

"But I can't give you what you want, intimately," Pandora turned her head, embarrassed. "I haven't touched anyone in almost three years. I'm not ready ye-"

"That doesn't matter to me," he cut through her confession, "we will wait as long as you want." His hands drifted up her legs, needing to touch her again- to wipe the past from her mind, wanting so badly for them to be together again. Standing up in front of her, he brushed Pandora's lips with his. They were warm and puffy from her crying, but to him, they felt like paradise. He pecked at them gently at first, asking permission. It took her a moment, but finally, she kissed him back. Their energy penetrated through skin, through flesh, and into the cells of their body. Pandora's small hands gripped his towel, pulling him further into her, owning him the way she always has.

"You're mine, baby," his eyes burned into hers, as her fingers traced his jaw, "*Forever mine.*"

"Yes, *yours.* They don't get to keep you, Bruce. *No* other girl gets to be who I am."

"And I don't care where this crazy life leads us. You'll *always* be mine," he confessed, as they stood in the room kissing each other with a rough possession-sealing the words.

Chapter 4

Present Day

Two female law school students sat in a briefing room of the Virginia Beach courthouse recording a live trial that Pandora was in the middle of working. Both students came equipped with their laptops to take notes, but neither of them could manage to type down anything because their eyes were glued to the screen watching Pandora like a hawk. She was defending a man named Robert Price who was charged with the first-degree murder of a Pastor. After a heated, ongoing altercation between Robert and the Pastor, Robert showed up to his church one <u>Sunday morning</u> and put a bullet in his skull just as he had gotten up to preach.

"No way in hell is she gonna win this case," Miranda shook her head, watching the screen in awe with a slacked mouth.

"Agreed," Sofia nodded, "the prosecution is eating her alive in there."

"Well, in her defense, this is a hard case. I heard no other law firm would touch it, out of fear of it defiling their reputation."

"Which is exactly what Anna is about to do," Sofia laughed.

The Judge called for a fifteen-minute recess, and the entire courtroom began to disperse. Dressed in a pair of high waisted gray slacks and a black silk bow tie neck blouse, Pandora gathered her belongings and grabbed her briefcase. Her mid-back length curls danced behind her as she glided out of the courtroom, gaining the attention of every man present. The second she walked into the briefing room, Miranda and Sophia jumped at their laptops, pretending they were taking notes the whole time.

"Hello ladies," Pandora beamed.

"Hey," Sophia hesitantly looked up.

"I'm sorry I couldn't get you guys into the courtroom. I tried my best, but this judge is cutthroat and wouldn't budge."

"Are you alright this morning?" Miranda chimed in, "I don't think I've ever seen you so nervous before."

"Is who alright? Me?"

"That prosecution is fierce, and the Judge along with most of the jury members are men. How the heck are you gonna pull this off?"

Pandora tilted her head back and laughed. "Has law school taught you *nothing*? I've already pulled it off. As a woman in a courtroom full of men, I have to be as feminine as they would like a woman to be, but at the same time possess the wit and sharpness to my personality that lawyers are known for. I didn't come on strong at first because I don't want them to feel threatened," Pandora gestured with her hands, "when you threaten a man's ego, *especially publicly*, they'll fight extra dirty and devour you. But if I sit pretty and play nice they'll assume I'm not as tough as they heard, and won't work as hard."

"True," Sophia nodded, " but they're making you look like a fool out there. Even your client has the look of defeat all over his face."

"Correction. I'm *allowing* them to make me look like a fool out there," Pandora smiled, "trust me, honey, I am as cunning as a fox and deadly as a black mamba. I got this."

"Watching an actual live trial is different from the ones we've seen on Law and Order. For this to be such a high profile case, I was a bit bored at first."

"Get used to it. This field isn't as exciting as you've probably imagined. Especially not in the beginnings of a trial. Before you even see the inside of a courtroom there's a lot of research and case law referencing to back up your arguments. You'll spend your evenings and weekends writing hundreds of legal briefs filled with a bunch of semantics," Pandora opened up her briefcase and took out some paperwork to show them. "And once you get in front of a judge, it's basically just laying out the facts for the jury piece by piece. And remember, one of the first rules I taught you'll is-"

"*In selecting who to pick to decide your fate, always advise your clients to pick a jury, not a judge,*" Miranda and Sophia responded in unison.

"Exactly," Pandora playfully slammed her fist on the table. "It's a miracle to get twelve people to agree on a place to eat lunch, let alone the guilt or innocence of a defendant." Miranda and Sophia broke into laughter.

"But do you really want to be judged by a bunch of people who weren't smart enough to get themselves out of Jury Duty?" Miranda asked.

"That's *exactly* who you want judging you. Juries are made up of people who are unfamiliar with the law. People like that can be easily swayed by lots of elements that have absolutely nothing to do with the facts of a case. For instance, if a jury likes a defendant they'll have a hard time convicting them of a charge that could put them in a cell for the next twenty years."

"Is that why you make most of your clients show up in nicely pressed suits rather than the usual prison orange and handcuffs?" Sophia took notes on her laptop.

"Yes, ma'am. And that is precisely why Casey Anthony's wardrobe and hairstyle was carefully chosen in an attempt to make her appear sweet and innocent. I mean, sure, juries are *supposed* to be impartial and base their judgment on the evidence presented, but human nature doesn't work like that." Pandora stood up and hit the rewind button on the DVR, allowing Miranda and Sophia to see all the male jurors gawking at her as she pranced out of the courtroom. "The likability of the defendant's legal counsel also carries weight," she grinned.

Miranda and Sophia shook their heads and burst into laughter.

"I'm serious. If an attorney is sloppy, grumpy, or boring, the jury is less inclined to believe a thing they have to say. On the other hand, if the lawyer appears to have their stuff together, is well-spoken, and yes- *good looking*, they're more inclined to believe me, and by extension, believe my client."

"You are conniving. I love it."

"Oh, you have *no* idea," Pandora squinted devilishly. "Toward the end of a trial is where all the excitement comes in. *This* is when you get to be entertaining and show the crowd a good time. The system is boring, but you don't have to be.

"Yeah, we've seen you in action plenty of times," Sophia chuckled, "Every time I watch you on television I can always expect objections and out of orders."

"That's how you do it," Pandora proudly smirked. "I run my mouth to the point where they have to pound the table and bang the gavel to shut me up. Just before the Jury deliberates, that's my moment to come alive and show every male ego in there that I've got a big swinging penis too, and I'm not afraid to use it," Miranda and Sophia just stared at her, trying to take it all in. Every law student from Virginia to Maine wanted a chance to intern for Pandora's law firm, but she never allowed it, until now. Pandora got up and grabbed a drink of water from the fountain, just as the court began to come back from recess. Walking over to the mirror, she adjusted her blouse and re-perfected her hair before spinning around to face her interns.

"Pay attention ladies," she playfully grinned. "I'm only gonna show you this *once*."

Mirada and Sophia watched through wide eyes looking like kids in a candy store. Pandora grabbed her briefcase and walked out of the room. You could hear the clicking of her shoes echoing down the corridor. She moved like a trained bloodhound ready to crush her competition under the heels of her Louboutins. A few minutes later, the doors of the courtroom opened and Pandora strutted through with a type of reverend energy that almost made you stand up and bow down. She walked with freedom and sass, her posture poised and confident, and her hips swayed with every step she took.

"Mrs. Ford, if you're ready, you may proceed with your closing arguments," the Judge ordered.

"Thank you, your honor," She walked up to her table and sat her briefcase down. She didn't bother to go over any last notes or pay the least bit of attention to the prosecution's demeanor. She glided over to the front of the courtroom, meeting the Jury's collective gaze with a contemplative expression. "*The next time I see you, I'm gonna cut your dick off and shove it down your throat,*" Pandora paused, briefly making eye contact with everyone. "*Just wait you bastard. When I see you again you'll be begging me to kill you.*" She paused again, raising an eyebrow at the jury. "*When I leave my pulpit on Sunday, I'm coming down your row to lay hands on you.*" These are the words from a *pastor,* the man the prosecution claims, is a *victim,*" she made air quotes with her hands. "You've seen the text messages sent by Pastor Gregory to Robert Price for yourselves. You've heard Pastor Gregory's wife admit under oath that she watched in fear while he sent them to my client. That doesn't sound like a *victim* to me." All eyes followed Pandora while she paced the floor. "They sound like serious threats, and where I come from, threatening to chop a man's penis off, them's fightin' words." A series of low chuckles filled the courtroom. Bracing her arms on the railing box of the jury, Pandora glanced at each one of them, making them feel included. The Jury tried their best to focus on her words, but most of them couldn't help themselves from staring into her honey brown eyes. They were mixed with copper and captivated them like sunlight shining through whiskey. They were mesmerized and trapped under her spell. Right where she wanted them.

"Over the course of this trial, you've heard things about my client, Robert Price, that are abhorrent and unflattering. I'm assuming you don't like him very much, and to be honest, I'm not too fond of him either. He had an affair with a married woman, the wife of a pastor. Not only that, when she refused to see him again, he disrespected her and posted nude photos of her, all over social media. As a woman, hearing such accusations were offensive and appalling to me. They're certainly not the actions of an honorable man, and if he were being judged on human decency, I certainly wouldn't be defending his honor." Pandora straightened her posture, capturing their rapt attention once more, "but we're not judging him on human decency. You are here to judge Robert Price's actions on the morning of <u>September 24th.</u> We as a society don't usually penalize individuals for defending their lives from physical harm, and that's exactly what Robert Price was doing on that morning. My old debate coach always told us that a smart offense is the best defense. Robert Price came face to face with a man who threatened his life relentlessly, giving him every reason to believe those threats would be carried out," she paused a final time, letting her words sink in. Finally, Pandora took a step back and addressed the jury as a whole. "So as you deliberate, I'm confident that you will conclude my client acted in self-defense, and render a verdict of not guilty." Before taking a seat at the defense table, she put the finishing touches on her argument. "Thank you for your time and attention. You've all been...*delightful.*" She smiled innocently, showing off her perfect teeth and ocean deep dimples. That got smiles and flirtatious stares from nine out of the ten jurors. Throughout the entire case, Pandora acted as if she were timid and shy, allowing herself to be walked over and cut off whenever she tried to speak. Suddenly when it mattered, she came to life and won over her audience in a way the prosecutor *knew* he couldn't compete with. The prosecutor was so angry, you could almost see steam flying out of his ears. Pandora walked back to the defense table and took her seat while the jury began their deliberation.

"Nailed it!" Jackson discreetly wrote on a legal pad and slid it to her. Due to the severity of the case, Pandora was given extra security to protect her whether she won or lost. She was seated in the midst of four large security guards, but Jackson always made sure to act as her personal escort whenever it was necessary. Grabbing her pen, she wrote back, *"I learned to "nail" from the best."* Pandora was a consummate professional and didn't even crack a smile as she passed him back the notepad. *"Speaking of nails, my hind parts still have your nail marks on them,"* Jackson internally grinned like a schoolboy. She read the notepad and allowed herself the barest of grins. *"Does that turn you on?"* Pandora was in the middle of one of the biggest cases of her career, and

her husband was being inappropriate and completely unprofessional. But that's what made things so much fun. The fact that her client and everyone else in the front row could just glance over and see what they were writing, added to the thrill.

A mischievous sparkle lit up in her eyes while she scribbled: *"You turned me on the second you walked in here with that double-breasted tailored suit. Now stop."* She rewarded him with a subtle smirk, and that was enough for him. After almost two years of marriage, Jackson still felt like he was on a honeymoon.

Pandora was powerful, dominant, and fearless within her career, but marriage had taught her how to separate business from pleasure. Little by little, she began peeling off the outer layers of her façade and grew more comfortable allowing Jackson to see who she really was. The second she walked through her front door, she allowed him to see the sweet, vulnerable side of her that was often hidden from the rest of the world. He had become her safety zone and he loved every bit of it. With the help of Quinn, Pandora mastered the art of submission. She made Jackson feel like she needed him, and she was a woman that never needed *anything* from *anybody*. Her weakness for him boosted his ego and drove him crazy. Jackson appreciated every inch of Pandora, and then some. He lost himself in her every single day. All the people he murdered and the lives he'd destroyed was worth it all in his eyes.

Suddenly, everyone in the courtroom grew silent while the forewoman rattled off the case number and read through the charges. Finally, she uttered the magic words: "*Not guilty.*" Robert Price got up with heartfelt eyes and extended his arms to hug Pandora.

"You are an amazing woman. Thank you so much, Anna." Pandora got up from her seat, surrounded by her bodyguards, and extended Robert an unyielding handshake, keeping him out of her personal space. The family members of the pastor, however, went into an uproar. They began shouting, cursing, and damning Pandora to hell. The pastor's brother tried diving over the defense table to attack Robert, but he was quickly taken down and arrested.

"No problem." Pandora was grateful she won her case, but after what happened to Eden, she was overcome with guilt knowing she played a significant part in getting criminals like Robert out of hot water. As the uproar in the courtroom began to elevate, Pandora and Robert were quickly escorted out of the courtroom, and outside, being met with angry churchgoers, protestors, and national news media. Jackson and the rest of the bodyguards were so busy protecting Pandora and her client from the front, they didn't even see the pastor's elderly mother roll up behind them in her wheelchair.

"God has the final say!" She pointed angrily at Robert. Pandora spun around, causing all of the bodyguards to jump in front of her.

"Ma'am, you aren't allowed beyond that yellow police tape over there," Jackson furrowed his eyes at the elderly woman.

"It's alright," Robert ushered Jackson out of the way, "She deserves the right to speak her peace. She's harmless." Robert knew what he did was wrong. The least he could do was allow the Pastor's mother to get some closure.

"Then she can speak her peace when *you're* alone," Jackson darted his eyes at Robert, "My wife is standing here and this woman isn't allowed to be within fifty feet of this defense, so she needs to back up-*or get backed up.*" The other guards walked over to usher the woman away.

"I don't like you either, *girl*," the woman's eyes narrowed into razor-sharp slits, glaring at Pandora. The news media and paparazzi flashed their cameras in the direction of the ongoing drama, trying to be the first ones to broadcast the scene.

"Yes ma'am," Pandora nodded, unaffected, "such kind words from a Christian woman. You have a good day." The guards began to wheel the woman away.

"You remind me of Satan, just slithering on in to trick Eve out of Paradise." Pandora gawked, blinking her eyes at the woman. She'd been called some pretty harsh names in her career, but never the devil.

"I'm so sorry you feel that way," Pandora grimaced.

"I know your brother, Joseph, too," the woman's crooked finger jutted out at her. "He's such a fine specimen of a man. Handsome, polite, kind. He's a good boy," he glowered at Pandora again. "Not like you. *Satan.*"

A slight flush swept across Pandora's cheeks just as the woman was wheeled out of sight. Pandora was embarrassed, and deep down her feelings were hurt. She was able to play it off quickly enough before the news media flashed their cameras and microphones in her face.

"Such nice words from the family of the prosecution, Joanna," a newscaster said, amused, "Looks like her words may have gotten to you. Any regrets?"

"Absolutely not," Pandora spoke confidently, "to be an effective criminal defense counsel, an attorney must be prepared to be demanding, outrageous, irreverent, blasphemous, a rogue, a renegade, and a hated individual," she winked with a devilish smirk, "very few people love a spokesperson for the despised and the damned."

"Congratulations," another newscaster stuck a microphone in her face, "this is the tenth win in a row for your firm. Do you have anything to say to the families of the victims?" Pandora glanced at her watch.

"That's all the time I have left for questions, guys. I have another important engagement I'm late for." Pandora turned around to face Robert. "Good luck out there. You're gonna need some added security. I'll have my guys escort you down to the station for your things. From there, you're on your own." Robert nodded and mouthed a swift, "Thank you," just as the remaining bodyguards swarmed around him and the newscast began bombarding him with questions. Jackson rushed over to Pandora and walked swiftly alongside her as she headed back into the courthouse.

"You're leaving a client high and dry?" He asked, confused, "Are you alright?"

"Yes, I'm fine," she declared through rushed speech, "Superwoman is done for the day. I have to get to the rehabilitation clinic."

"Rehabilitation Clinic?"

"Yes, silly," Pandora hurried down the corridor and out the back door toward her car. "It's <u>February, 3rd.</u> Eden's coming home today," she gleamed. Jackson choked on his spit.

"That's- that's *today*?" He hesitated, slowing down his pace while he watched Pandora frantically fish for her car keys. "I thought you said she wouldn't be out until at least the end of Fall, if at all.

"No," she winced, unlocking her car door, "unless I just forgot to fill you in on the updates. She's been progressing along faster than expected. She made a full recovery and they're letting her come home." Jackson grabbed the handle to Pandora's Aston Martin, opening the driver's side door for her to get in. He could feel his pulse beating in his ears, blocking out every other sound except the ragged breath moving in and out of his body. The last time he heard, Eden had severe brain damage and although she had come out of her coma, the doctors threatened that she might be a vegetable for the rest of her life. She was expected to be released sometime in the Fall. Closing Pandora's door, he rubbed a hand down his face before walking over to get in on the passenger side. "I'm a little annoyed that I'm just finding out about this," he put his seatbelt on, trying to keep his hands from trembling.

"I'm sorry. With you being in and of town over the last couple of months, and me working myself to death over this case, I haven't had much time to communicate with you."

"Well, you should have made time!" A sadistic tone laced his voice, causing Pandora to snap her head in his direction.

"I said I was sorry, *geez*," she frowned, confused.

"You've never shown much concern anyway. For the last eight months, you've been trying to force me to get back to normal. Every time I brought Eden up, you found a way to change the subject. I just assumed that was your way of coping, so I left you alone about her."

"That's not true. Look, I'm sorry, okay? Her coming home so suddenly just caught me by surprise that's all. You were really going through it in the beginning, and things didn't look good for Eden at first. I was just trying to push you back to the woman you were before the accident in case we lost her," Jackson lied.

"And that's fine. I didn't complain about it. I'm grateful for it because I needed that extra push. But anyway, a lot has changed within the last four or five months. The doctors assumed she'd be a vegetable, but they couldn't give us an exact diagnosis until the swelling in her head went down. Turns out, there was no bullet lodged in her skull, it only grazed it. It went through her ear, so they did surgery to fix the nerve damage and a bunch of other things. Of course, she still needed to learn how to walk, eat, and be normal again after her body suffered through so much. But as of right now, she has her full mind," Pandora's voice weakened and tears began to spill from her eyes. "She's gonna be okay, and she's coming home."

If Jackson was standing up, he probably would have fainted. His legs felt like they were paralyzed. He could almost see his life flashing before his eyes. In his mind, he was one hundred percent sure that Eden was on her way to death, and he was patiently waiting for that moment so he could get on with the life he had killed for to build with Pandora. All the pieces of his deadly, sick game had been taken care of and there were no traces of evidence that pointed back to him. *Except Eden.* He had no idea what Travis may have told her. He was never supposed to fall in love with her to begin with. Travis's only mission was to befriend her at school, drug her, and kill her, but he dragged things out for months and complicated everything. Now that he was dead, Jackson had no way of knowing what all he'd said and done to Eden. Jackson sat in the passenger seat of Pandora's car sweating like a sinner in church. A feeling of dread crept into the pit of his stomach and he almost vomited his lunch all over Pandora's dashboard. Eden coming home in her right mind was not in his plans, and he now had to think quickly to finish what he started.

Chapter 5

Surprise!

Eden sat on her bed beside Quinn in her temporary bedroom at the Northern Virginia Rehabilitation Center, lacing up her sneakers.

"Do I *really* have to go out in public like this," she cringed, gazing down at her orthopedic white sneakers.

"It could be worse," Quinn concealed her laugh, "you could be going into a public area full of people you know."

"If my mom were here she'd be laughing herself silly at this wardrobe."

"Oh, don't worry, Anna will make up for it when she gets sight of you."

"I can't wait," Eden darted her eyes at Quinn. Dressed in a Wal-Mart brand gray sweatshirt with matching pocketless sweatpants, Eden stood up and gave herself an overview in the mirror. Ten months prior, her face was barely recognizable, and today, she was on her way home. Although the hospital hadn't given her the best attire, she felt fortunate to see her old self staring back at her. After being shot and beaten, the first two months of her hospital stay were terrifying. Eden fought through multiple surgeries to reconstruct her eardrum, broken nose, broken jaw, and fractured skull. Once she was healthy enough to be released from the hospital, she was admitted into an inpatient rehabilitation center to further assist in her recovery. For eight months, Eden worked through rigorous bouts of therapy to help with pain management and regaining the independence of her limbs. Trained specialists worked around the clock to assist her in building strength, mobility, and fitness. The occupational therapists were available to help push her back into her daily activities, and the speech-language therapists assisted her with speaking, understanding, and learning to write again. Although Eden had physically escaped the hands of an abusive relationship, her emotional uphill battle to normality had only just begun. She needed the help of a trained psychologist to get through it. Aside from being her best friend, Quinn's skills and expertise made her the best person for the job. *"In order to ever be whole again,"* Quinn held Eden *while she cried her eyes out, "you have to release your denial and accept the hand life has dealt you. The trick is to integrate all of those awful things into who you are without allowing it to define you."* Pandora, while she was no psychologist, knew a thing or two about rewriting your entire self-concept. She taught Eden how to include her victimization without allowing herself to be a victim. She helped her unlearn all of the unhealthy coping strategies she used to get herself through a season of torment with Travis. Pandora taught Eden to replace things such as being overly submissive, silent, second-guessing herself, and beginning every sentence with "*I'm sorry*." Together, both of her friends resuscitated her sanity and bought her back to reality. The more comfortable Eden grew within her own skin, the quicker her mind healed.

Eventually, she got rid of all the self-hatred she felt for allowing herself to suffer so much and learned how to fully forgive herself. Travis had implanted in Eden's mind that she wasn't loveable, but with practice, she learned to square away the hatred and re-learn that she was worthy of love. Lastly, through talking, support, and the unwavering love from Quinn and Pandora, the three of them spent the final months of Eden's hospital stay restoring their broken friendship. With Quinn being a mother, Pandora being a wife, and Eden suffering through a life-threatening tragedy, the three of them fully understood that life had taken them down separate roads and changed them. They each found more production in meeting one another where they were, instead of trying to cling to the way things were before. This allowed them to build a stronger version of the closeness and intimacy they once had.

"Mannequin, what do you think of th-" Eden spun around to ask Quinn a question, but furrowed and crossed her arms when she noticed Quinn laughing profusely at her attire. "Really?"

"I'm sorry, but you look like a pledgee trying to get into a sorority with those sweatpants and medical sneakers."

"So," Eden placed a hand on her hip, "I still look good."

"You do. *Pledgee.*"

"Whatever, Quinn," Eden shook her head and giggled, just as the doctor entered into the room.

"Looks like somebody's ready to get out of here," he walked over and extended a hug to Eden.

"That somebody would be me," Eden accepted the hug and smiled at the six foot three, middle-aged, handsome doctor. Dr. Goodrich had a butter pecan complexion. His strong jawline, salt and pepper hair, five o'clock shadow, and ocean blue eyes had given Eden a new appreciation for white chocolate.

"Oh, hi, Dr. Bentley," He turned around, noticing Quinn. He immediately blushed at the sight of her. "It's always nice to see you."

"It's nice to see you too," Quinn smiled gracefully. Dr. Goodrich stood stapled to the floor, staring at Quinn like he was starving and she was something to eat.

"I'm sure you have a wife somewhere that would slap you right now for staring so hard," Eden joked.

"Who me?" he laughed, breaking himself out of his trance. He didn't realize he'd made himself that obvious.

"Yes, you Dr. McDreamy."

"I'm engaged actually," he admitted, "but that doesn't stop me from appreciating beautiful women from time to time. To be honest, I've grown pretty fond of all three of you in these last eight months. Ya'll are certainly more interesting to watch than these senior citizens and recovering addicts." The three of them shared a laugh, "But honestly, your recovery here has been a miracle, Eden, and I don't use that word too often. I've never seen anything quite like it. Consider yourself blessed."

"Indeed, she is," Quinn affirmed with a swift head nod, "God has been good to her."

"You know, I'm not really a man of faith anymore, but Eden's progress has certainly dared me to believe again."

"I was never really religious or spiritual myself," Eden admitted, "but this past year has shattered my belief system and changed my perspective of God. There's no way I could believe he doesn't exist anymore."

"I'm so proud of you," Quinn smiled.

"My mom used to tell me that often times, God will use a tragedy to get our attention. I never really understood it at the time, but after going through what I went through, I have a lot of questions as to why."

"Ruby was right," Quinn nodded, "I always say it's best to come to God when he calls you. Don't make him have to come get you."

"Well that sounds *evil*," Dr. Goodrich raised an eyebrow, lowering himself on the edge of Eden's bed, "why would a good God purposely allow humanity- that *he* created, contract incurable diseases and tragedies just so we'd believe in him?"

"My point exactly. Take me for example," Eden pointed to herself, "If God wanted to get my attention, why not just put it in my ear to go to church or something? Why did I have to meet death and suffer the way I did?"

"I agree," Dr. Goodrich chimed in, "I had a mother of Jewish faith who put all of her trust and belief into a God that ultimately allowed her to suffer from cancer and die a long, painful death. I gave up my belief in Judaism after that."

"Well, to be brutally honest, we were birthed into a sick, dying world, and those are just some of the many issues living in a less than perfect paradise will bring you," Quinn raised her eyebrows. "Like bullets, pain and suffering have no names on them. Every disciple that walked in the name of Jesus, including Jesus himself was unfairly persecuted and died horrendous deaths."

"I never considered that," Dr. Goodrich nodded with a pensive expression, "But why? Why persecution and death versus long life and prosperity to those that believe? There's a scripture somewhere that states no weapons formed against the believer would prosper."

"Correct," Quinn affirmed, "God never said they wouldn't *form*, he promised they wouldn't p*rosper*. Adversity, anguish, trials, tribulations, heartaches, and yes, *even death*, are valuable lessons of experience in our lives. Death wakes people up. Broken hearts bring us to a higher level of insight and understanding. Tribulation has a way of changing our perception of the world around us and forcing us to be better people." Eden nodded in understanding. Dr. Goodrich pinched his lips in deep thought for a minute, before staring at Quinn in amazement.

"You know, you have a very practical way of sharing your insight about Christ. Where do you go to church?"

"Tabernacle Church of God in Christ. You're more than welcome to come one Sunday. Bring your fiancé along, too."

"I think I'll do that. Will you and your husband be present?"

"Something like that," Quinn winked with a smile that caused Eden to snicker.

"Great. Well, Eden, I'm so sorry we had to meet on such horrible terms, but I'm very happy we did," Dr. Goodrich got up from the bed and handed Eden her discharge papers. "You have an amazing support system, and the things I've watched you accomplish in the last ten months, I wouldn't have believed if I hadn't seen it for myself," he smiled. "You're free to go."

Eden's eyes lit up like she had hit the winning Powerball. She took her discharge papers and stared down at them, smiling from ear to ear.

"I should get going. I have other patients to see. You ladies enjoy the rest of this beautiful day, and hopefully, I will see you on Sunday?"

"That would be awesome," Eden waved, watching Dr. Goodrich exit just as Pandora entered the room with a devilish grin.

"Is she using Jesus to pick up men again?"

"No, I was *not*," Quinn gawked, welcoming Pandora with a hug.

"Yes, she was," Eden rebutted, "just like last month when she had that sexy custodial worker begging for the church address."

"A few weeks ago it was a state trooper on the way back from the beach," Pandora narrowed her eyes at Quinn.

"You two are such troublemakers. It was *nothing* like that."

"Quinn, the man let us out of a speeding ticket and treated us do dinner."

"Whatever, he was just being nice," Quinn chuckled.

"*Mmhm*," Pandora shook her head and dropped her purse on the desk, "anyway, I'm sorry I'm late. I had that big trial today."

"We saw on the news," Eden replied, "We thought you'd never make it out of that press conference alive. *Satan*."

"Please. I wouldn't have missed this for the wo-" Pandora spun around to face Eden, and choked on her words when she realized what Eden was wearing. She quickly turned her back and burst into laughter.

"Ugh," Eden muttered, turning around to gather her bags.

"Eden," Pandora turned to face her friend, the look of confusion was all over her face, "you look *ridiculous.*"

"They wanted her to wear the orthopedic sneakers home," Quinn forced herself not to laugh about it anymore.

"You guys, can we just get out of here so I can take this crap off," Eden asked, impatiently.

"Yes, we can," Pandora smiled, pulling Eden into her arms, "I'm so happy you're coming home. I've been waiting for this day for months."

"Me too," Quinn joined in. They both took a good long look at Eden, extremely proud of everything she'd accomplished.

"Alright, let's hit the road," Pandora said, excited. They helped Eden gather the rest of her belongings and made their way down the hallway to the exit.

"Where are we going anyway? You never did tell me."

"It's a surprise," Quinn replied. "You'll see when we get there."

"No, really," Eden said as they walked outside to Pandora's car, "I have no phone, no home, no clothes, no-"

"Eden, just get in the car," Pandora protested.

"Okay, but if I don't ha-" At the sight of Jackson stepping out of the passenger side, Eden stopped dead in her tracks. Her smile quickly vanished.

"Hey, Eden," Jackson hesitated with a warm smile. Eden swallowed, dry-mouthed. She was not prepared to run into Jackson's conniving, murderous behind the day she was being released back into society. *He was the reason for her being there in the first place.* There were quite a few things she wanted to say to him. *Hey* was not one of them. "What's wrong? Cat got your tongue?" Jackson joked.

Eden simply nodded, tossing him her bags before quickly disappearing into the back seat.

"What was that all about?" Quinn frowned.

"I don't know," Pandora replied with a puzzled stare.

"Did I do something?" Jackson turned to face Quinn and Pandora, "I mean, other than being an old flame and former baby daddy, I guess," he laughed nervously, taking Eden's remaining bags from them and placing them in the trunk.

"I suppose."

"Babe, the office just called. I have to make a run, so I'm gonna head out with Abe," Jackson quickly kissed Pandora's forehead.

"Oh, is that who that is in the truck?" Pandora smiled, turning around with a swift wave to Jackson's partner.

"Yeah. I'll call if I'm gonna be late getting back."

"Great. See you soon."

"Good seeing you Quinn," Jackson smiled and waved, quickly rushing to get into the truck behind them.

"You too, honey," Quinn waved back, getting in the passenger's side of Pandora's car, as Pandora followed. "Gosh, do you two *ever* sit still and enjoy each other's company?"

"About thirty percent of the time," Pandora laughed, pulling off, "Maybe forty percent if you count holidays and sick days."

"How does that work out? Don't you'll ever miss one another?

"Absolutely, we do," Pandora winced, "It's just that we both have very demanding careers, so time is never really on our side.

"I mean, me and Andre are constantly on the go as well, but we're *always* together. I couldn't imagine just seeing him in passing," Quinn shivered, dreading the thought, "Even though we're busy, I'm comforted in knowing that when I look to my left, I can see his face."

"That would get on my nerves," Pandora chuckled. "I love Jackson to death, but I also love what I do. Over the years, I've become so engulfed in my career that I'm used to my space, you know? One of the things I feared about marriage was having to downsize, and with him, I don't have to do that because he's just as busy as I am. When we do get together after a week of texting and FaceTime, our intimacy is stronger, the lovemaking is more fulfilling, and our hearts have grown fonder toward one another."

"So, what do you do about sex when you can't see him?"

"Don't you ask me that," Pandora gasped, embarrassed, "mind your business," they both laughed. Eden sat in the back seat with her arms folded. Her eyes rolled back and forth like dice. She had no idea how long she was supposed to keep quiet and allow Karma to get Jackson back. Jackson's intent was to kill her, but he'd failed. What would stop him from trying again? And what about

Pandora? Eden knew Pandora could handle her own, but knowing she shared the same bed as a murderer and had no idea of it made her fear for Pandora's life as well. Through a trembling hand, Eden wiped the perspiration from her forehead, as fear coursed through her veins. Just as she turned to look out the window, Ruby's words of wisdom ran through her mind. *"Vengeance is not yours to give or think about giving. Let it go, and live."*

"Honey, you okay back there?" Pandora's voice broke through her thoughts.

"Yeah," Eden blinked her eyes, shifting her mind back to reality, "I'm just anxious to get to where we're going."

"Just a few more minutes," Quinn promised. Pandora's phone chimed loudly in her purse.

"See who that is, please." Reaching into Pandora's purse, Quinn pulled out her cellphone.

"Hopefully my client didn't get sodomized and stoned on the way out of court," Pandora nervously clutched the steering wheel. As Quinn read the text message quietly, a slow-building grin formed on her face, quickly gaining Eden's attention.

"Who is it? What's it say?" Eden anxiously leaned toward the front seat. Quinn bit her bottom lip, trying her best to conceal her smile. Staring straight ahead, she robotically raised her hand to give Eden the phone.

"Who is it?" Pandora momentarily took her eyes off the road to glance at Quinn.

"Oooh," Eden read the text message to herself, a devious smirk formed on her own face.

"Give me my phone," Pandora reached behind her and snatched the phone from Eden's grip, glancing at the text message.

"Baby, I've been calling you all morning. We need to talk, ASAP. It's important.
–Bruce."

Pandora fixed her eyes on the text message, taking her eyes off the road. Suddenly, the sound of car horns blaring loudly forced her to refocus her attention and realize she was swerving into another lane. She gasped, barely dodging a collision with another vehicle.

"Geez Louis, Anna," Eden sat back and reached for her seatbelt.

"I'm sorry," Pandora tossed her phone back into her purse and swallowed, focusing her attention on the road.

"You alright?" Quinn snickered, moistening her lips.

"I'm *fine*," Pandora declared, annoyed. She could feel Quinn and Eden's eyes asking all types of questions.

"Will you take those silly looking grins off your faces?" She fussed, "I know what ya'll are thinking, and it's *nothing* like that."

"I didn't even know you and Bruce still communicated."

"We don't- well, we've had brief interactions since Eden's accident. He wanted to make sure she was okay, and for me to tell her he said hello."

"Hellooo, detective," Eden smiled flirtatiously, "Quinn, I guess this answers your question as to who's satisfying her when her husband's not around."

"Stop it," Pandora grimaced.

"You didn't tell us you two were friends," Eden teased.

"We are *not* friends."

"Then why is he saved in your phone?" Quinn tilted her head.

"*And* on a first name basis this time," Eden chimed in, "in college she had him saved under Idiot."

"Will the both of you cut it out," Pandora glowered, dismissing her friends' accusations.

"Relax," Quinn rubbed Pandora's leg, amused by her growing irritation, "we're just joking. But seeing his name brought back so many memories of you two."

"Yes," Eden reminisced, "I swear they were the cutest couple ever. My mom loved him."

"My heart literally broke for both of them after high school. I love *love*, and they were the epitome of it."

"But wait, you guys got back together in college, and then two years later you broke up for good and never told us why," Eden perked her posture up.

"I didn't believe it until Andre and I got an invitation to his wedding a few years later," Quinn chuckled. A brief silence filled the car as Quinn and Eden patiently awaited an explanation.

"Am I really being harassed about something that happened ten years ago?" Pandora huffed.

"Yes," Eden and Quinn replied in unison.

"We need closure," Eden chuckled, "you guys were everything."

"Life happened," Pandora admitted. "We dated for a couple years and then he cheated on me, so we broke up and that was that. I went to law school, and he went into the academy and got married."

"That doesn't sound like Bruce to cheat," Quinn squinted, "at least not on you."

"Well, I guess there's a first time for everything."

"I wonder why he divorced his wife. They seemed so happy together on Facebook. His daughter is beautiful."

"He told Andre his heart wasn't in it and that he was tired of living a lie," Quinn proclaimed, "I'm sure there's more to the story, but I guess we'll never know."

"Well he's engaged now, so I would assume his heart works just fine," Pandora bit her tongue. She knew she was the sole reason behind Bruce's divorce, but sleeping with a married man and tearing apart a family was a mistake she swore she'd take to her grave.

"*Engaged,*" Quinn and Eden gasped in unison a second time.

"He doesn't sound engaged in his text message, *Baby,*" Eden teased.

"Whatever, well I'm happily married and uninterested in some old flame."

"Unless it's still burning, of course," Eden smirked.

"Nothing is burning," Pandora replied through clenched jaws. Eden took her finger and placed it on Pandora's cheek, quickly snatching it away like she'd just touched a hot plate.

"Lies. You're burning up," Eden joked. Quinn roared with laughter. Although she was annoyed, Pandora couldn't help but giggle at her crazy friends. Surely, she was over Bruce. That's what she convinced herself, and whether she liked it or not, that's what it was going to be.

"We're home," Pandora broke through the laughter as they pulled up to the driveway of a newly built, red brick, two-story residence.

"Whose home?" Eden's mouth dropped open, gazing at the beautiful property through the window. The house had columns, friezes, and arched windows twenty feet high. It looked as if it had been designed with the imagination of Picasso. "Did you move again?"

"No," Quinn grabbed her purse as Pandora turned off her car and got out, "But you did." Slowly, Eden opened up the car door and stood in awe at the breathtaking sight in front of her.

"Ho-ly, crap," were the only words she could think of. Quinn and Pandora both walked over and wrapped an arm around her with a smile, soaking in the scenery from Eden's vantage point.

"Quinn and I had it built for you while you were away. It's directly in the middle of both of our homes," Pandora smiled, "We tried to get Miss Ruby's house back, but the new owner wouldn't budge, so we figured this would be the next best thing. I hope you like it."

"Do I?" Eden rushed to the front door, "Let me in!" They gave her the keys and she unlocked a front door that looked like it could accommodate a family of giraffes. The second they walked in, the smell of fresh paint hit them, as did the spacious open floor plan. Eden walked around slowly, taking in the scenery. The floors were polished stone with a large white Persian rug to accent it. The pink and caramel furniture in the living room looked as if it had just come straight from the warehouse. Tears of gratitude filled Eden's eyes as she walked through the place, staring at all of the pictures and poems on the wall that reflected her values, beliefs, and passions. It looked as if her friends had read her mind and created her a hideout from humanity and the threats of the world. Eden walked upstairs to a large master bedroom, fully furnished. Inside of the closet were brand new clothes and shoes that her friends had purchased for her. Overwhelmed with joy, Eden turned around and nearly leaped into both of their arms.

"Thank you guys *so* much," her voice shook, "I can't believe you did all of this for me."

"Eden, we would do anything for you," Pandora wiped a tear from the crack of her eye, "You've been through a lot, and we're here to help you."

"We also re-purchased Miss Ruby's hair salon and coffee shop. We got them up and running to make sure you have a steady stream of income. I have an accountant handling everything now, but the minute you're ready to learn the ropes and take over, feel free to do so," Quinn smiled.

"Seriously?" Eden's eyes gaped open.

"Seriously," Quinn affirmed.

"Wow, this is…this is unreal. A house, an income, new clothes. What else do you two have up your sleeve?"

"Well, we did consider how you may feel living alone and since we can't be here 24-7, we thought you might like a roommate," Pandora's eyes glittered with excitement.

Eden turned to face them, narrowing her eyes, "A roommate?"

Quinn and Pandora glanced at one another with eyes that sparkled and gleamed, unable to contain their final surprise any longer. Suddenly, the master bathroom door swung open and Eden went pale, raising a hand to cover her racing heart. Jade stood in the doorway with a wide grin plastered on her face.

"Surprise. Hey roomie!"

Chapter 6

"Dear Heart, Why him? – Anna"

It was a little past eight pm and after helping Eden unwind and settle into her new home, Pandora parked outside of her office and jumped out of the car. She'd completely forgotten about her meeting at the US Attorney's office earlier in the day. Her upcoming client, a forty-five-year-old man name Dunkin Howard, was charged with pimping and pandering. He was responsible for recruiting prostitutes into the sex industry, soliciting money from them, transporting them to and from hot spots, and advertising their sexual services. If Pandora couldn't get him off, he would be found guilty and sentenced to over a decade in prison. He'd also have to pay thousands of dollars as monetary punishment. After completing his legal brief, she realized there were no loopholes to getting him off the hook, so her next move was to engage in the rudimentary, behind the scenes activity that keeps the court system from grinding to a halt; *negotiating a plea deal*. She knew Dunkin was guilty, and the prosecutor knew it too, but it was her job to convince them to take the easy win, a lesser charge, and a reduced sentence. After all, it saved the taxpayers money.

"He connects people with the same interests, is all," Pandora explained, rushing through the parking lot behind David Bradshaw, the prosecutor on the case, "He looks for people who are looking for specific attributes in a partner. The ones who don't have the time to scout out a potential companion."

"Diplomacy at its finest," David shook his head, "Also known as bull crap. I left my dinner table to come meet with you. You'd better give me something better than that. Howard is a pimp. Point blank, period."

"He's a matchmaker," Pandora argued, as they entered into her office building and stood in the vestibule.

"Right," David laughed, "and next you'll be trying to prove that drug dealers are pharmacists."

That's actually not a bad argument, Pandora thought with a chuckle. *I may use that in the future.* "My point is, Howard isn't working with under-aged girls, crossing state lines, or abusing these women. This is a harmless victimless fish, and you've got a whole sea of sharks to fry. If this were Nevada, it wouldn't even be a crime."

"Well then, big homie should've set up shop in Nevada," David rebutted, "I can lessen his charges to tax evasion and procuring."

"We'll take the tax evasion, but not procuring, *come on.*"

"Joanna, you're forty five minutes late. I'm supposed to be at my dinner table right now, and you're still trying to bargain?" He laughed with a headshake.

"I'm sorry. I got tied up helping out a friend. But if my memory is correct, the last time you needed me, I got your son out of some scalding hot water and I didn't give you a hard time about it," she raised an eyebrow and pursed her lips. David furrowed, giving Pandora a long, agitated stare before finally giving in.

"You're lucky I love you like a sister. We'll go with tax evasion. But I want jail time. That bastard will not skate on probation or house arrest."

"How about a low-security facility?" Pandora pushed the envelope one final time.

"Deal." David held out his hand, allowing Pandora to shake it.

"Great. Now get back to your wife. I'll go up right now and get the legal brief done and fax it over to your office. You'll have it first thing in the morning."

"You be careful hanging around this late, alone," David replied, concerned, "Do you want me to wait around for you?"

"Please," she retorted, "I'm never alone. I have some company in my purse." David shook his head and grabbed his keys from his pocket.

"What? A container of mace and some pepper spray?" He laughed. "Like I said, be careful. You're too pretty to be out here this late."

Pandora shyly laughed, dismissing his feministic comments. "I will do that. And thanks for meeting up with me so late." She reached for her purse to answer her ringing cellphone, giving David one final wave before she headed toward her office door.

"Joanna," she answered sweetly.

"Hey, it's me," Jackson replied, "I'm home and you're not."

"Hey baby, I'll be there in about an hour, I had to run to the office to fax over some paperwork."

"Can't wait. You hungry? How about Red Lobster tonight?"

Pandora unlocked her office door and walked inside. "I'd love Red Lob-" She stopped dead in her tracks, nearly jumping out of her skin when she saw Bruce sitting at her computer, peering up the second he saw her. "*Finally.* You are a hard person to track down," he grinned.

"I'll call you right back," Pandora hung up her phone, barely waiting for Jackson to respond, "What the hell are you doing in my office?"

"A few years ago it used to be you," he licked his lips. "All across this desk."

Pandora's nostrils flared, as she reached into her purse. Bruce stood up and rushed over to her knowing exactly what she was getting ready to pull out. "I'm just kidding, relax," he laughed. "I texted you earlier and told you I needed to talk to you. You didn't answer, so I figured you'd be in your office. You always work late on Wednesdays."

"So you break into my office and go through my computer?" Pandora fussed, flinging her arms out.

"I wasn't going through your computer," he defended, "I was playing solitaire to kill the time. And I didn't break-in. I still have your spare key," he raised an eyebrow, dangling the key in front of her. Pandora snatched it out of his hands.

"The next time you need me, I have office hours Monday through Friday, nine to five," she hissed, "and my name is Joanna, not *baby.*"

"Listen," he walked into her and rested his big hands on her shoulders. "I think we may have gotten off on the wrong foot, I'm sorry. We were friends for a long time so forgive me for failing to keep things strictly professional. It won't happen again."

Pandora glared at him, and gosh, he was magnificent. His eyes were a brown so dark they were nearly black. Thickly lashed, they were intensely gorgeous. Suddenly, she felt bad for being so rude, and the familiar scent of his cologne was causing her mind to travel elsewhere. Blinking herself back to reality, she backed away and put her game face on.

"It's alright. How can I help you?" Dropping her purse on a nearby chair, Pandora walked over to her desk. She turned to face him and his eyes trailed her beautiful face. He remembered her soft lips and soul-stirring kisses. He caught wind of her mesmerizing, relentless brown eyes. Had he really thought they were soft and warm? There was nothing soft about Joanna Ford. She was a hard, jaded woman, cut from a ruthless cloth. *And he loved her.* Bruce watched in distraction as her crimson-tipped fingernails skimmed through the papers she held. "I have to—" he quickly gathered his thoughts, "I have to get going soon, but I've been doing some heavy research and my findings have opened up a case; a case that you'll be working alongside me on considering your knowledge of the victim."

Pandora almost snapped her neck the way she looked up at Bruce. "What type of case? And why do I have to—"

"You said your office hours are Monday through Friday, nine to five," he raised an eyebrow with a smug look on his face, "if you can pencil me in for one thirty, I'll come correct tomorrow with all of my paperwork and logistics."

"I have court at noon," she sighed, crossing her arms. "I can meet with you at 3."

"3 is fine. I'll see you then. *Joanna,*" he gave a swift nod before turning to walk out of the door. The second it closed behind her, she flopped down at her desk. Working alongside Bruce was how she got into this mess to begin with...

Charlotte, North Carolina, - Seven years ago

Bruce sat at a table reserved for him and his wife at the thirty-fifth annual banquet dinner. The event was always held on the last day of the Attorney General's networking retreat in Charlotte. Over the course of the weekend, there were different activities and chances for lawyers from across the country to introduce themselves and enjoy a weekend of skill-building, workshops, and sharing meals with other brilliant minds. Connections were built, partners were created, and friendships were made at the retreat every year. As a detective, Bruce was never really interested in that sort of thing, but with his wife Angela in her final year of law school, he thought it might be good to connect her with some good people. He was also excited to take a break from his never-ending workdays to finally spend time with her, away from their one-year-old daughter.

"Thank you so much for bringing me here," Angela gleamed, looking around the room in amazement, "this is like paradise for a law student."

"I figured you'd like it," he gently rubbed her leg. "Some of the lawyers here are linked to multi-million-dollar firms, and if you can find a way to connect with them, you'll set yourself up for greatness."

"What do I say?" She faced him, partly embarrassed. "Would they look down on me as some imposing law student?"

"Absolutely not," Bruce winced, "you're here with me. Everybody knows me. The ones from some of the California districts, I do favors for all the time and they'll be glad to take you under their wing."

"If you say so."

"Sweetheart, just relax. I promise you'll do fine," he gently kissed her forehead as the chief of police walked over to their table.

"Detective Steed," he belted out, "I thought that was you from across the room!" Bruce turned and immediately got up, his handsome face lit up with excitement.

"Chief Sidney," they firmly shook hands, "How's it going?"

"It's going," the chief laughed, "I haven't seen you since the academy, but I've heard how much of a beast you are. I'm so proud of you."

"Just trying to be like you," he blushed, sliding back so the chief could see his wife, "Chief, this is my wife, Angela. Angela, this is Chief Sidney. He's the one that got me into the academy."

"Hi, nice to meet you, Chief Sidney," Angela stood up with a smile, extending a warm hug. Removing his hat, the Chief stood in awe of Angela's five foot six, Latino supermodel frame. Her strong cheekbones and waist-length auburn hair caused Chief Sidney to give her a slow, once over.

"The pleasure is all mine, Madam. I'm so sorry I missed the wedding. I had every intention of being there. I heard you have a daughter too."

"Indeed," Bruce proudly pulled out his wallet, displaying pictures of their daughter.

"My goodness, you've been busy boy," the Chief's belly shook as he laughed.

"Angela is just finishing up with law school, so I thought this would be a good place for her to begin networking."

"Oh, sure. This place is crawling with good lawyers from all over the country." Bruce reached down to grab a napkin just as the Chief looked to his left, "as a matter of fact, here comes one of the best right now. She's only been here for about two years, but she's already made partner and hasn't lost a case yet.

"Oh my," Angela looked on in awe.

"She'd be great to talk to. Actually, I just pulled some strings to get her on your next case, Bruce. Anna?" The Chief yelled, gaining Pandora's attention, "Come over here a minute." Bruce looked up from the table and it was as if he was having an out of body experience when he saw Pandora turn to walk in their direction. Dressed in an elegant, form-fitted, knee-length black dress that highlighted every hill and valley of her petite frame, Pandora glided toward them with a walk that could've put Tyra Banks to shame. She'd grown up since college. Her figure was fuller and more defined. Her hair was longer and lighter, but she would always be that girl that took Bruce's breath away. Bruce could feel his pulse elevating at the sight of his first love. The closer Pandora got, the slower she appeared to be moving, because she too, noticed Bruce at the table. After reuniting in Bruce's dorm room, Pandora and Bruce's relationship picked right up where they left off before she was kidnapped. They spent every waking moment together, and Bruce protected Pandora's heart as if it were made of a colorless diamond. He attended counseling with her to help her overcome her fears of sex, anger, low self-esteem, and older men that reminded her of Mr. Perkins. Bruce maintained a life of celibacy, patiently and proudly waiting until Pandora was ready to take that next step with him again. He couldn't wait to graduate so they could get married. Although Pandora made it known to him that she'd be unable to ever have children due to her reproductive system being destroyed, Bruce was okay with it and they talked about other ways of starting a family through adoption or fostering. They were head over heels in love with one another, flaws and all, and it seemed like nothing would ever tear them apart.

One night after football practice, Pandora lay drunk and naked in her bed, waiting for Bruce. She'd planned on breaking her celibacy and wanted to surprise him. After an hour of waiting, she finally gave up and texted him a picture of herself in bed. She begged him to hurry up, and to wear his football helmet and uniform tights she loved so much. Bruce soon came into her room, and they ended up making mad, passionate love...at least she thought it was Bruce. Eventually, the real Bruce did come up to her room, and when he saw her pleasing another man that looked to be one of his teammates, he nearly fainted. He couldn't believe that after two years, she'd cheat on him and give herself away to someone else. Angry, resentful, and bitter, Bruce decided that he'd never love again.

The next day, Pandora walked into Bruce's room to find him having a threesome with two members of her debate team. At the sight of his infidelity, Pandora felt her heart re-shatter into pieces while Bruce looked up at her with a smirk. She turned around and stormed out of his bedroom, and that was the end of them. Graduation happened almost a week later, and both of their shattered hearts had officially gone their separate ways. But no matter how hard he tried, Bruce could never forget Pandora. Her love almost seemed to be engrained in his genetic makeup. She was a big part of who he was and he spent the last four years looking for a woman to make him feel like she could.

Finally, he found Angela, and while she couldn't measure up to Pandora, she made him happy in her own way, so he got married and started a family. Pandora was different. Throughout law school at Temple, she remained completely in control of her heart. Bruce did cross her mind a few times, but she would quickly replace his face with a memory of something else. She wasn't interested in love or settling down, but she did have a few friends to satisfy her sexual needs when she needed them. After all, flings were all she had time for in law school. The closer Pandora got to Bruce, it seemed as if the last four years without him hit her like a ton of bricks. It felt like the room had disappeared and their souls were levitating toward one another. What they had was unforgettable. *And unfinished.*

"Joanna," Chief Sidney ushered Pandora over by her waist when she'd gotten close enough," this is detective Bruce Steed, he works in the fifth precinct in California. He's who you'll be working with on the Jamison case." With a wavering smile, Pandora extended her hand, "Hello, detective."

"It's a pleasure," was all that managed to escape Bruce's lips. They both locked eyes with one another, unable to form a complete thought. Bruce shook Pandora's hand and it felt like fireworks on the Fourth of July.

"And this is Bruce's wife, Angela," Chief Sidney broke through their trance. Pandora blinked thoroughly, making sure she heard correctly. Wife? "She's a law school student in her final year and Bruce brought her to network. I thought you'd be the perfect one to mentor and show her the ropes."

After a brief pause, Pandora forced a smile. "Absolutely, hi Angela."

"Hi Joanna," Angela replied nervously.

"I was actually just getting ready to head out back. They have a rock band out there playing. Care to join me so we can chat?" Angela widened her eyes and sucked in a quick breath.

"Sure." She quickly stepped out from the table and proceeded to walk away with Pandora. "Honey, I'll be back in a little bit." Bruce just watched with an unfocused gaze, unable to speak.

"Cat got your tongue?" Chief Sidney laughed, giving him a slight elbow to break him out of whatever spell he was under. Indeed, the cunning kitten had his tongue. She had his heart as well.

"Sure, honey," he scratched his head and swallowed, "see you soon." Bruce watched them walk away and the minute they were out of his sight, he sat down and rubbed a hand down his flushed face. This could not be happening to him right here right now. Bruce was married with a brand new baby. He told himself he found love, and that Pandora was a thing of the past. So why did the very sight of her make him wanna jump across the table and snatch her into his arms?

"My goodness, you see that woman?" Chief Sidney whistled, eyeing Pandora like she was a piece of meat. "I swear, every officer in my precinct has tried to take a stab at her," he laughed, "but she's not budging."

"No. I didn't notice," Bruce lied, reaching for his phone to look distracted.

"What are you, blind?" Sidney laughed, "Those curves are dangerous. I'd crash trying to drive something like that now, but man, if I were fifteen years younger, I'd-

"That reminds me, whatever happened to that woman we found dead after she drove her car off of Snake Hill? Did we close that case?" Bruce purposely changed the subject. He hated hearing another man talk so loosely about Pandora. He never put up with it in college, and for some reason, that same jealous temper was still there. As Chief Sidney rambled on for the next thirty minutes, Bruce zoned out. His mind raced a million miles per minute, and it had nothing to do with the dead woman on Snake Hill, or his wife. His thoughts were consumed with Pandora. He needed a moment to talk to her. He wanted to hear her voice and he couldn't wait a minute longer.

"Chief, I'll be right back, I need to make an important phone call," he lied, getting up from the table.

"Sure thing. It was nice talking to you, son, I'll see you around before the night is over." They shook hands, and Bruce dipped off as fast as he could, making his way out back.

Outside…

As the rock band blared loudly, Angela sat at the bar getting acquainted with Pandora, periodically pausing to watch the show. For almost forty-five minutes, she rambled on and on about her loving husband and their brand new baby. She talked about her goals after law school, and her future plans to give Bruce more children. There was no room for Pandora to get a word in edgewise to even *try* to mentor Angela. She seemed to know it all and had it all together. Pandora was surprised Bruce would marry a woman like that, let alone have children with her. Although Angela was beautiful, she seemed far from his type. The more Pandora listened to Angela's rant, the more her mind drifted off into the distance trying to get a grip on reality. Was this really happening? Was the man she swore she would spend the rest of her life with since junior high, married to someone else? He had a baby and started a life without her? Was this real? Her heart seemed to grow sluggish with each question. All of her suppressed feelings were now on the surface and it hurt like hell. She wanted to cry, she wanted to scream, she wanted to slap the hell out of Angela so she would shut up. Pandora's brain felt like it would explode if she sat there another second. Just as Angela ended one subject and was getting ready to go into another one, Pandora jumped up from the barstool.

"I'll be right back," she elevated her voice over the band, "I'm gonna use the ladies' room."

"Okay, do you want me to walk you?"

"No-No" Pandora said quickly, "I'll just be a few minutes."

"Okay, I'll be here when you get back." Pandora turned and broke free like a runaway slave. She didn't know where she was going, but she wanted to get as far away from Angela as possible. She had no idea where the ladies room was, so she scurried to the end of the courtyard behind two large trucks the band used to carry their equipment. Once Pandora was hidden, she leaned against the truck, took in a deep breath, and exhaled a cry. She covered her mouth and tried to catch herself, but tears began plummeting down her cheeks to a point where she couldn't control it.

"Hey," a deep, remorseful voice filled her left ear. Pandora spun around quickly, looking like she'd just gotten caught with her hand in the cookie jar. Bruce felt a rush sweep over him as her teary brown eyes met his. He felt weightless, and everything else in the world seemed to disappear.

"Hey," Pandora wiped her eyes as best as she could.

"Why are you crying?" He slowly paced his way over to her, caressing a hand down her cheek.

"I'm not...I just-" lowering her head, Pandora hid the ongoing stream of tears that wouldn't stop flowing. Being around Bruce for just a few seconds was already causing her brain to feel out of sorts, and it made her uncomfortable. In Pandora's life, everything had to be in order and under her control, and Bruce did not fit into that order. She wanted to turn and run away from him as fast as she could, but her feet felt rooted to the cement so she just stood there and cried.

Bruce moved in front of her and wrapped his arms around her. With a finger, he lifted her head and took in the sight of her beautiful face. Her eyes were closed, her mascara ran, and her panting lips quietly sobbed, releasing heart-shattering sounds of disappointment and regret. If Bruce had any talent for painting, that would have been the masterpiece he would've captured; a pure, unguarded moment when the woman his heart had broken for stood completely bare before him. He had so many questions to ask her. He wanted to know how she was doing, where she lived, and how life had been treating her. Was she married? Did she have those adopted children yet? Was she in love with someone? Was he treating her right? His eyes darted to her lips and he wondered what they'd feel like after four years. If he didn't land on a thought soon, his head would explode. Finally, he couldn't contain himself. He knew he was married and that his wife was nearby, but in that moment he would've thrown it all away for Pandora. Cupping her face into his hands, he reached down and kissed her. Pandora's eyes popped open just as she felt his body pushing hers against the back of the truck. Bruce's touch was so powerful it left her breathless and unable to do anything but stand there and take what her heart wanted. Wrapping her arms around the back of his neck, they kissed passionately, roughly, as if their next breath depended on it.

"I miss you, baby. Come back to me," he panted, running his nose up her cheek, listening to her breath escaping in tiny puffs. Pandora forced herself to stay controlled, but Bruce was so clever with his touch she was having a hard time formulating any type of coherent thoughts. After two years of marriage, Bruce and Angela didn't have much intimacy anymore, and when they did it was pretty uninspired. Their love life had become entangled with all the conflicts, hidden emotions, and disagreements that had accumulated over the years. Their feelings were bound by the struggles for possession and power over the other, bringing all of the intimate terrorism into the bedroom with them. But this...this is what he'd been searching for since college.

 Bruce sucked and tugged Pandora's bottom lip, skimming up the outside of her thigh, taking her dress along for the ride. He tasted her neck, kissed her cheek, and made his way back to her soft lips. Her heart slammed wildly through her chest, and her skin burned everywhere Bruce touched. They both stood trapped within one another, engulfed in tenderness, passion, and inflaming kisses.

"Do you want me?" Bruce rasped, teasing his tongue up the soft part of her throat. Pandora moaned, forgetting where she was.

"Yes," she begged in his ear. The sound of her plea was like a gun going off at an Olympic race.

They'd been waiting years for this moment...and here it was. Pandora snatched his belt off and ripped the clasp that secured his pants to get what she wanted; she didn't have time for buttons.

"Everything was so wrong, but it felt so right," was the last rational thought Pandora had before Bruce picked her up and leaned her against the back of the truck as they made wild, animalistic love in a passionate, egoless state, seizing a moment that didn't belong to them. They pushed and pulled on each other until it was over for them. The screaming heavy metal band hit its crescendo at the same time Pandora did, allowing her lungs to scream. When it was all over, they gazed at each other, helpless and satisfied as the music died down and reality slowly sank back in. Cupping the back of her neck, Bruce placed a passionate kiss on her lips as he gently placed her feet back on the ground. They both breathed heavily, gazing deeply into each other's eyes.

"What the hell did we just do?"

Chapter 7

The next afternoon, Jackson headed into Pandora's office building carrying a bouquet of all of her favorite flowers. Red roses, white daisies, and purple asters beautifully overcrowded a crystal vase, fashioned with a silk white bow. Jackson knew Pandora was on the verge of winning another case, and even though it was a low profile one, he loved surprising her with congratulatory flowers waiting in her office. Dressed in a tailored, precision-cut three button, blue suit, Jackson walked with a professional, yct casual stride to his wife's office door. His broad shoulders, dominant posture, and waist-length locs swinging behind him had all of Pandora's female employees sneaking glances as he passed them.

"Good afternoon, ladies," he smiled, opening her door.

"Hi Mr. Ford," some of them responded through their flirtatious giggles.

The second he closed the door and spun around, Jade gasped and stood straight up in Pandora's office chair.

"Whoa," Jackson froze.

"Hello," Jade gave Jackson an incredulous stare.

"Can I help you?" He tilted his head.

"Um, sure," she laughed nervously, stepping away from Pandora's computer. "You're Jackson, right? I'm supposed to be meeting with your wife. She's ten minutes late."

"She's still in court. But I'm pretty sure you're not supposed to be waiting for a meeting in her office. At her *personal computer*," Jackson furrowed, walking over to Pandora's desk to place the flowers on it.

"I'm actually her temporary assistant. She hired me last month. I was cleaning her hard drive."

"*Welcome, temp,*" he said nonchalantly, "but I doubt she'd ever give any type of assistant access to her private things." As Jackson walked around the desk to face Pandora's computer, Jade kicked the power cord out with her heel.

"Oops," she gasped, "I'm so sorry." Kneeling down, Jade quickly plugged the cord back in but before she could stand up, Jackson snatched her up by the arm and yanked her toward him.

"What the hell were you doing snooping through my wife's computer?" He gritted. Jade looked at Jackson with the fear of God.

"I was- I told you, I-"

"She's gonna have your head on a platter when she finds out. I told you to use *discretion* in this place. That was a horrible act." Letting her go, Jackson huffed.

"Jackson, relax," she rolled her eyes and jerked away from him, annoyed, "you give that barking dog way too much credit. She's in *court*. No one saw me come in here; no one knows I'm in here."

"Listen," he threatened, "I hired you to do a job, and I want it done *my* way."

"And I've done your job," she scolded, "I played the worried, concerned friend. I got in good with Quinn like you said, and it opened the door for Ms. Gullible to let me move into the house."

"How are things over there?" Jackson walked over to Pandora's door to make sure it was fully closed.

"It's hell," Jade flopped down in a nearby chair, "Eden is acting weird around me now. It's as if we were never friends. She barely talks to me, she's never at the house, and every attempt I make to hang out she declines with some crap excuse. I don't know what's up with her. She gave me a look when she saw me the other day, too," Jackson nodded, "I think she knows something." Jade looked at Jackson like he was stupid.

"*What,* that you hired my fiancé to kill her and now you've hired me to be your watchdog? Honey, if she knew that, she'd be giving you more than just a *look.* Relax. She's probably still adjusting to home life." Jackson thought about it for a good while before eventually nodding his head in agreement.

"You're probably right. And Anna hasn't been doing anything suspicious?"

"Other than being a self-absorbed, controlling wench?" Jade huffed in disgust, "No. She's been working on cases this whole time. I can't *wait* to get away from her. She doesn't like me at all, and the feeling is definitely mutual."

"I wouldn't take it personally. Anna has a hard shell."

"*Please.* She acts like she has a personal vendetta against me. You should see the way she stares me down, it's so creepy."

"That's just how she is. She's untrusting of anyone she doesn't know. You're guilty until proven innocent in her world," Jackson replied, amused, "Besides, I asked you to keep an eye on Eden. *You* asked me to get you in here."

"Because I'm trying to apply to med school and you told me she knew people on the Board of Trustees that could get me in," Jade's eyes darted at Jackson. "So I talked to Quinn like you suggested, and I inched my way in here so Anna could prep me and set me up for my interview."

"So then what's the problem?" Jackson raised an eyebrow.

"The problem is I've been here for three months, and other than her treating me like a second class citizen, she's barely prepped me. I applied on my own and my interview is in a few weeks."

"Just be patient," Jackson looked at his watch, "Anna does things on her own time, but when she gets it done, she gets it done. Trust me." Jade stood up and pranced over to Jackson, wrapping her arms around his neck. "Seems like she hasn't been getting *you* done," she seductively licked down his earlobe, "you seem so tense." Jackson certainly couldn't hide his sexual frustration. With Pandora working long hours, and Jackson traveling all week, they hadn't made love in almost five days. For a man like Jackson who was used to being pleased around the clock, he was *certainly* feeling the dry spell.

"It's been a couple of days," he admitted.

"I can tell," Jade grinned deviously.

"Jade," Jackson's voice was full of guilt, knowing just what she wanted. He was a murderer in love and hated the thought of cheating on his beautiful wife. After all of the orchestrating and manipulating he'd done to get the woman he craved, the *least* he could do was be faithful to her.

Jade had a different motive in mind. She always knew who Pandora was, and when she discovered Eden was best friends with her, she worked her magic to try and be close too. Jade didn't realize Pandora rarely had a heart that allowed outsiders into her personal space. Since she couldn't be Pandora's friend, she ended up despising her and hating her with a passion.

After working for Pandora, Jade became jealous of her power and envious of her success. Sleeping with Jackson whenever she felt like it gave her a sense of validation and allowed her to feel like she had one up over Pandora. In order to keep Jade content and quiet while he figured out his next move, Jackson allowed it. Pushing him against Pandora's office door, Jade dropped to her knees and took what she wanted. Just as they were finishing, Jackson heard a familiar clicking of heels and infectious laughter walking toward the door.

"Shoot!" Jackson's eyes popped open.

"Just play it cool," Jade quickly stood up and fixed her hair.

"Are you *crazy?!* I don't want her ever seeing us together. In her mind, we don't know each other and it *has* to stay that way." He quickly adjusted his pants, ran for her closet and jumped inside. "Find a good excuse as to why you're in here," he ordered. The closet door slowly shut and Pandora's door unlocked.

"I can't do the twenty-fifth, that's the lawyer's retreat," Pandora held her phone to her ear and used her free hand to push her office door open. "I *did* tell you. It's in D.C this year so I'll be leaving a day early to get some time in for myself." A man in his late thirties walked in behind her. She walked over to a chair and flung her purse onto it.

"Great, we can reschedule for the following da-" Pandora turned toward her desk and saw Jade standing beside it looking like a deer in headlights. Furrowing, Pandora looked at Jade and then turned to look at her door.

"Right. Listen, we'll chat later on, Susan. Take care." Pandora hung up the phone and refocused her attention on Jade, blankly staring at her.

"Hey," Jade tried her best not to appear nervous, "your husband was just here with these," she pointed to the flowers on Pandora's desk, "he was in a rush and told me to snip and water them for you, but I guess," she laughed nervously, "I guess you can do it yourself since you're here." Pandora crossed her arms and glowered, impatiently waiting for a better explanation. This intimidated Jade.

"Also, we were supposed to meet at no-"

"Please don't come into my office uninvited, *ever* again," Pandora bit.

"I'm sorry, I was doing what -"

"I don't care what you were doing. First off, let's clear the air here," she pointed a finger in Jade's face, "I *do not* like you. We are not *friends* and we are not a*ssociates*. You are *the help*, and a favor for Quinn."

"Wow...You certainly have a way with words," Jade snorted, masking her embarrassment.

"So I've been told," Pandora strutted around to her desk to look at her flowers from Jackson.

"Well, like I said, I'm sorry and it won't happen again. I'll see my way out."

"Actually, you can stay for a second. I bought someone in for you to meet." Pandora motioned the tall lanky brown skin man over to her desk. "This is Dwayne. He's a longtime friend of my firm. He's also one of the admissions officers for the Virginia School of Medicine."

"Good afternoon young lady," Dwayne walked over and extended his arm. Partly shocked, Jade rushed over and extended her hand to Dwayne.

"The pleasure is all mine," she blushed. Dwayne was easy on the eyes as well and tickled her fancy.

"Anna has spoken very highly of you for some time now. She told me you applied for an interview with our school so I thought I'd come out and meet you myself." Jade jerked her head back, partly shocked before turning to stare at Pandora.

"*You* spoke highly of *me*?"

"I spoke highly of your work," Pandora retorted, lowering herself into her office chair. "You're a good assistant."

"Oh wow," Jade looked back at Dwayne, "I'm not sure if being introduced to you, or getting a seal of approval from her is more compelling."

"Joanna is...*Joanna*." Dwayne assured. "She is cutthroat, but you're in good hands."

"Anna, thank you so much. You have no idea how much this means to me," Jade clasped her hands together, smiling at Pandora, "I was a bit leery of all of this at first. You told me you'd help me with med school, but this whole time I've been a paper pusher and an errand girl. I was beginning to worry."

"I'm a lawyer, honey. I know people, but medicine is not my field. What I do know is that all of the admissions officers use the medical school interview to identify candidates with maturity, empathy, and superior interpersonal skills," she gestured, "they already know your credentials, it's on paper. They want to know what kind of person *you* are."

"Absolutely," Dwayne nodded, "and your paper pusher and errand girl skills show me that you're humble. Your ability to take a good thrashing stands out as well- it shows me that you're moldable and respectful." Jade smiled so hard, all thirty-two teeth showed.

"This is amazing. Thank you both."

"Well, I have to get going ladies. Jade, it was a pleasure meeting you." Pulling out his card, Dwayne handed it over to her. "Call me if you have any questions." Jade glanced at his ring finger and noticed it was bare.

"Actually, I have *several*," she flirted with her eyes. "Maybe we could meet up for dinner...a business dinner...if that's alright." Pandora tilted her head and parted her lips in disbelief.

"Dinner would be great," Dwayne gave Jade a slick once over, and nodded, "give me a call in a few days, we'll set something up."

"I certainly will," Jade blushed, watching Dwayne walk out the door.

"Well if you wanted to *sleep* your way to the top, you could've saved yourself the trouble of interning for me," Pandora rolled her eyes, opening her desk drawer.

"I am not sleeping my way to top," Jade devilishly grinned, "but he's sexy. Besides, being a woman in a man's world, *especially* within the lawyer- doctor realm is hard for strong women like us. Showing your boss that you have the power to be *powerless* helps you land your dream job quicker," Jade confidently strode over to Pandora's mirror, getting way beside herself. "I've seen your husband around. Don't tell me you've never bowed down on your knee pads to give up your power once in a while," Jade slyly turned and smirked at Pandora.

Pandora watched in silence for a second to make sure she was hearing correctly. Finally, she stood up and made her way over to Jade like a lioness scouting out its prey. "I'm never powerless, honey, even on my knees," she glared, "I *give*, my husband *takes*. But he *needs* me to give. He's d*esperate* for it. *Peasants* bow. Not Queens."

Jade sighed, annoyed and crossed her arms. She was sick of Pandora's intimidating ways. She'd finally gotten what she came for and planned to take things into her own hands to get where she wanted to go from here. Jade saw no further need to hide her true colors and kiss Pandora's behind.

"Are we done here, *Queen*," Jade mocked.

"Listen, I'm trying to *help* you," Pandora stated, "but you seem to have your own agenda, so, I'll let you take over from here. However, be very careful mixing business with pleasure. *Everybody* has a story to tell, including Dwayne. If I were you I'd keep it professional."

"Well, you're *not* me," Jade struck back, confidently. Pandora looked at Jade like she could claw her eyes out at any second. A knock at the door broke her death stare. "Come in-" Pandora declared.

"Anna, Detective Steed is in the conference room waiting for you. I can tell him your meeting with-

"Tell him I'll be right there. Jade was just seeing herself to lunch," Pandora stated with a coldness.

"Actually, I just ate lunch," Jade winked, "but I need to finish my work, so I'll get back to my desk."

"Awesome," Pandora impatiently ushered Jade to the front door, following behind her. "What did you have?" *Your husband*, Jade thought to herself, as a Grinch-like smile formed on her face. "Some nuts and a protein shake," she quickly turned the corner and made her way back to her desk.

"Everything alright, Anna?" her receptionist asked, sensing Pandora's irritation.

"Yeah, just had to put someone back in their rightful place," Pandora swiftly followed her receptionist to the conference room.

"Enjoy," the receptionist opened the door and walked away.

"Thanks, Candace," Pandora smiled and bounced through the open door of the conference room. "*Hello, Detective,*" The seduction in her voice set Bruce on edge. Immediately, he stood up to greet her.

"Good afternoon," he pinned her with his gaze and his heart began to race. Dressed in a huggable black pin-striped pantsuit, Pandora was ferocity dipped in elegance. She looked like perfection veined with flaws. Her power was unmistakable. The way she carried herself and the authority she wielded with faultless control made it impossible for her to ever fade into the background. They both stood within arm's reach of one another, trapped in an awkward moment of whether they should hug or shake hands.

Bruce smiled through his chills and reached out to pull her into him, but she quickly stepped back, pulled a chair out, and sat down.

"What can I do for you?" Swallowing his pride, Bruce rubbed his neck and sat down next to her. The lack of a welcoming kiss or affectionate embrace rubbed him the wrong way. The Pandora he knew and loved would have never done either of those things. She looked at him like a lion tamer circling a lion; cautious and watchful, but very much in control.

"Don't look at me like that, Anna," he ordered.

"I beg your pardon?" She sat back and raised an eyebrow.

"*Joanna*," his eyes threatened. Ignoring his remarks, Pandora looked at her watch.

"I want you to know that there's a three-month waiting list to get approved for any services coming out of my office. I have clients on top of clients, and I'm only one person. You're jumping in front of about fifty people. This had *better* be worth my time."

Anger began to build in Bruce's eyes, as he rubbed a hand down his frustrated face. He never did do a good job of hiding his emotions. He glared as if he could break something- like her face. Pandora, however, was appeased. This pissed him off. She had proven so many times that she could disappear from Bruce's life and never look back, while he could barely breathe without her. There was a fundamental imbalance in their relationship that always gave Pandora the upper hand, and he resented it. But since she'd gone out and gotten married, maybe she *was* officially over him. Refusing to put himself out there any longer, Bruce laid his emotions to rest, fixed his stature, and reached for his manila folder.

"I apologize," he bit coldly. Anyway, getting down to business. I've been doing some heavy research since Eden's accident."

"What kind of research?" The sound of Eden's name quickly caught her attention.

"Our boy, Jeremiah. Remember when we worked his case before? I arrested him for the murder of his mother, girlfriend, and the unborn fetus."

"*Okay…*"

"Jeremiah was an undergraduate business major. After he was acquitted, he moved to Chicago, finished his bachelor's, and then obtained a Masters in Business Administration from an online school in South Dakota." Bruce handed Pandora the paperwork for her to sift through. "He graduated within a year and a half, and next, I found records of him attending a school in Chicago for a Ph.D. in Business. There were also some old bank loan forms showing him trying to borrow money to open up a few barbershops along the east coast. The banks declined him because he didn't have enough credit history."

"So what's your point?" Pandora sifted through the papers, confused.

"I'm getting there, *wait,*" Bruce said impatiently. Pandora bit her lip to hide her amusement. "Jeremiah also was a hitman. Since his arrival in Chicago, there have been several missing person's reports of collegiate aged girls who still, to this day, haven't been found. I also found a private bank account of his," Bruce pulled out another folder and passed it off to her. "Ironically, after all of those girls popped up missing, there were huge money transactions placed into his account." Pandora listened intently as her eyes trailed up and down Bruce's paperwork.

"I looked up that *same* account during the time frame of him and Eden, and I noticed several small transactions, but after Jeremiah was pronounced dead, the money was wiped clean." Pandora furrowed her eyebrows, putting the pieces together. "Lastly, if Jeremiah was obtaining a *Ph.D.* in Business somewhere in Chicago, what the hell would he be doing at Virginia State taking a masters level sociology class?" Pandora paused before her eyes darted up at Bruce.

"So, your saying-"

"Somebody hired Jeremiah to kill her," Bruce affirmed. Pandora gasped and clutched her chest as a rush of anxiety swept through her body.

"But why? Eden doesn't have any enemies. Not any that would hire a hitman to kill her," she winced, confused.

"I didn't think she did either, but you did say she was taking drugs. Could it have been a dealer she pissed off?"

"No," Pandora stated quickly, "Ruby left Eden crawling in enough money to last her until the afterlife, so it's extremely unlikely that she'd owe anyone money."

"Well, this is my reason for needing your help," Bruce closed his folder, "Jeremiah was *hired* to do a job and was killed in the process. The intended target, *Eden*, is not dead. That means the original orchestrator of all this is still on the loose, probably trying to find a way to finish what he started." Pandora's lips parted as she snapped her head up at Bruce.

Chapter 8

Later that evening, Pandora dragged herself through her front door and kicked off her heels. She dropped her purse and let her Louis Vuitton briefcase slide to the hardwood floors. The smell of her favorite food, Fettuccine Alfredo, danced in the air. Smooth jazz melted through the silence, while candles filled her living room to capacity. The warm glow from the fireplace accented the romantic vibe. It was obvious that Jackson had been busy in preparation for a romantic evening, but Pandora felt so obliterated, she didn't even notice. She flopped down on her white, Victorian-styled love seat and wiped the rest of her flow of tears. She'd been driving around for the last two hours trying to rid her thoughts of Bruce, and her brain needed sleep just like her car needed gas. Her head ached, her eyes burned, and her arms and legs seemed to be giving up on her. She couldn't remember the last time she felt this drained, and it was all because of *him*. He'd found a way back into her life and was destroying her perfect, controlled world, one emotion at a time. There was a bond between Pandora and Bruce, primitive and ancient. One that transcended definition. Bruce could take her and use her. She was his, and his presence made it known that it didn't matter how far she tried to walk away from him, or how much of a distance she tried to keep, his hand would always hold the chains that bound them together. And when it suited him, he would pull her back, because she belonged to him. *Forever Mine*.

Pandora fought so hard to remain professional and controlled earlier, and it had drained the very life out of her. Before she even made it into the conference room for their meeting, she felt Bruce before she saw him. As she walked toward his presence, the air around her surged with electricity. It was like the crackling energy that always heralded the approach of a storm. His entire being hummed with awareness, and she hated it. Pandora was a woman of prestige and power, but he handled her with such an authoritative aura, it made everything inside of her surrender. *All the time*.

When Bruce stood up to greet her, it was almost breathtaking how gorgeous he was. His body was full of strength, and his muscles sprouted veins in every direction. His dark skin looked like midnight, and his deep brown eyes took her in like the rapture. His full lips and strong jawline looked like an avenging angel had sculpted every angle of his body into a level of flawlessness. He captivated her. He mesmerized her world, and always made it hard for her to think rationally. But it wasn't just his outward appearance; it was also who he was on the inside that dazzled her.

Bruce had relentless energy, sharp intelligence, and power, coupled with a heart that was so tender. Pandora was addicted to him- heart, soul, and body. After going years without him, she now felt unstable and off-balance. She refused to hug him earlier, not because she was being mean, but because she knew it wouldn't equate to just a hug. Bruce never could *just touch* her. He engulfed her. His body was so much bigger and harder. She felt safe and cherished in his arms. Nothing could ever hurt her when he was around. She was able to drop her guard and exhale knowing that she was protected.

Bruce Steed was as deep and vast as an ocean current, and since the very first day they laid eyes on each other, she feared drowning in him. They needed each other to a degree that most would consider unhealthy. It was who they were, and what they had. It was precious, and Bruce wanted it back. Seeing him made her realize she wanted it too.

After locking up her office and getting into her car, Pandora's overwhelming thoughts consumed her mind until her world dismantled under her feet. Life kept tearing them apart for a reason, and Pandora swore to herself that the last time would be their *last* time. She sealed their fate by falling in love with another man. She was now a married woman, and her heart belonged to Jackson. *Or did it?* She warred with her mind until her tears took over and she nearly drowned in them. Quinn and Eden didn't know about her hidden life with Bruce after college, so she had no one to talk to. She felt empty, confused, and guilty. She was so wrapped up in her emotions, she didn't even see Jackson sneak up behind the couch and kiss her neck.

"Hey you," he greeted her.

"Hey," her stale eyes lifted to meet him.

"You look like crap. Everything alright?"

"Yeah," she hesitated, "its been a long day. My brain is fried."

"That's a first," Jackson sounded partly surprised, "well, for you anyways. Your passion and drive for this type of stuff has always amazed me. I would've freaked myself out a long time ago trying to do what you do." Pandora just smiled warmly.

"Did you get my flowers? I left them with your assistant. Sorry, I couldn't stay to give them to you myself," he lied, knowing darn well he'd done more than just *stay*. After a good time with Jade, Jackson stood trapped in Pandora's closet for almost three hours waiting for her staff to leave. Thankfully, Pandora sent everyone home and locked up early, otherwise, he feared he'd pee himself waiting to get out.

"I did" she nodded, "They were beautiful, thank you." She glanced around the room, finally taking a mental note of all the detail he'd put into creating the romantic atmosphere.

"This is nice," she playfully cut her eyes at him, "what'd you do?"

"What?" He chuckled, "when have I ever needed to do something wrong to be romantic?"

"I'm kidding. But it is a random weekday, and you're usually working late."

"I took a night off," he pulled her into his lap, "we haven't really spent time together this week. I know we're pretty content and understanding of each other's schedules, but you've been on my mind a lot. I miss you." Pandora searched for something meaningful to say, but all that came out was, "You too," as she looked away from him, trying to fight off the guilt.

"Are you ready to eat?"

"Not really, maybe later. I'm gonna go up and get ready for bed."

"Well I'm hungry, and you look pretty edible to me," he reached in and nibbled on her neck. The smell of her perfume still lingered after a long day, and being close to her began to turn him on.

"Come on, that tickles," she giggled with a smile. Jackson paid her no mind. Laying her on the couch, he straddled over top of her and began to kiss her. *Distraction.* That's what she needed. A distraction, because if she'd sat there a minute longer, she felt like she'd start crying again. Ignoring her continuous racing thoughts, Pandora wrapped her arms around her husband's neck and kissed him back. Jackson kissed and caressed her until he built her into a fever pitch, and she began to moan.

"*Bruce*," she whispered against his lips. He went to unzip his jeans but stopped in mid-stride.

"Excuse me?" He furrowed…Shoot…Her eyes popped open, quickly searching for something to save herself.

"Springsteen," she belted out, as Jackson lifted off of her, "Bruce Springsteen is headlining the conference this year."

"What are you talking about?" He looked at her through a pinched expression.

"The conference," she sat up and readjusted her blouse, "the one you're going to with me in DC next week, remember? Bruce Springsteen is supposed to be headlining the appreciation dinner."

"Joanna, I'm trying to set the mood and your thinking about some stupid rock concert?" He complained, "and since when do you like Rock?"

"I don't - well, I like him- since I was a kid, and I finally get to meet him."

"Well good luck, I won't be able to go anyway. I have my own conference to attend in Raleigh," he stood up, annoyed.

"What do you mean," she winced, "you promised me you'd go with me for weeks.

"Well work came up," he replied, heartless. "I'm sure your girlfriends will go with you."

"Jackson…"

Aggravated, he pulled out some pamphlets from his pocket and threw them onto the couch. "I'm going to take a shower. Food is warming on the stove if you get hungry." Pandora glanced at the little booklets and saw they were pamphlets on starting a family and trying to conceive. "*Not this again,*" she thought, standing up and reaching for his hand. "Is that what all this dinner and candles is about?" He snatched away from her and went upstairs into the bathroom.

"Jackson," she hurried after him, "why are you ma-" just as she reached the bathroom door, it slammed in her face. Jackson grabbed his grooming kit from the medicine cabinet, shaking his head in disappointment. He spent the entire evening cooking dinner and making sure everything was set perfect. He missed his wife and had every intention of spending the evening with her in his arms. He also wanted to talk about planning their family again. He'd been bringing up having children for months now, and she always strayed away from the discussion for some reason.

Jackson wanted to start a family and create a legacy, and he wanted to start it soon. He wanted to talk about changing up their work schedules to make more time for one another. He'd gone to some family planning classes and he was excited to hear what she thought about it. Instead, Pandora's mind was in the middle of Mars, thinking about some stupid Bruce Springsteen concert. Reaching over their freestanding shower, Jackson turned on the water and snatched off his shirt. The bathroom door opened and Pandora stepped inside. Jackson glanced at her, pausing with his hand on the fly of his jeans. Pandora went to speak, but Jackson's stature wiped her memory. Her hot gaze drank him in, soaking in his frame. Her eyes missed nothing and touched everything. *Her heart was so confused.* Finally, she took a deep breath.

"We need to talk."

"Go to bed, Anna."

"Not until I say what I need to say."

"I don't want to talk anymore. I'm taking a shower."

"Fine," Pandora walked out of the bathroom and returned twenty seconds later wrapped in nothing but a towel.

"What are you doing?" Jackson was just disappearing into the steam when Pandora let her towel fall. Jackson paused.

"I'm taking a shower too, then."

"Talking isn't what's going to happen if you come into my shower," he warned.

"Listen," her eyes lifted back up to his, "I'm sorry, alright. My mind is somewhere else."

"That's the point; your mind should be on me. I've been trying to talk to you about starting a family for almost 3 months and you keep putting me off."

"I'm not putting you off," she fussed, "I just don't think having children is in my future," she swallowed, immediately regretting her honesty.

"Excuse me?" He urged his neck forward, "what do you mean *your* future. We're married. This is *our* future, which means mine hangs in the balance as well."

"I told you when you first met me I wasn't too sure about children. You keep trying to change my mind and it's not gonna happen."

"What the hell, Anna," Jackson slammed the water off and snatched a towel off the rack.

"You cringe every time I take you around my family, you don't want kids," he threw his arms up in surrender, "I'm confused, what was the point of getting married?"

"I married you because you asked me to, and I love you. I shouldn't have to validate or change who I am to keep you," her temper ignited.

"Don't make this about me!" Fury sizzled through his blood.

"This *is* about you because every time we have a disagreement you bring up your pathetic family. I married *you. Not them.*"

"Well if you didn't want to deal with in-laws, you should've married an orphan!" he roared. Angry, Pandora grabbed her towel, spun around and stormed out of the bathroom. "Don't walk away from me." She flipped her middle finger over her shoulder and disappeared into the hallway. "Get back here," he marched after her, catching her in three strides. He grabbed her arm and spun her around. "We're not done." She shoved away from him. "We are done, and *now* I'm going to bed."

"You don't run this marriage and I'm tired of you talking to me like you do!"

"Ditto!" she roared.

"Gotdammit!" He lunged for her and she jumped out of the way. "What type of woman doesn't want children with her own husband!?"

"The kind that is barren and can't have any!" She screamed to the top of her lungs. Jackson froze. Pandora stormed into the bedroom and re-clothed herself. It took her words a couple of minutes to register in Jackson's mind.

"How long have you known this?" He finally walked into the doorway of the bedroom.

"Does it matter?"

"To me, yes."

"Long before you came into the picture."

"And all this time I've been mentioning kids, you kept something like that from me?"

"Would telling you that I couldn't have children prevented you from marrying me?" She looked at him.

"I don't-" he caught himself. "That doesn't matter anymore. I'm here aren't I?"

"Answer the question, Jackson," she folded her arms.

"I'm a family man. I want to leave a legacy, I-"

"*Answer the question.*"

"No!" He responded quickly. "Okay? No, I don't think I would've asked you to marry me." Cupping her mouth with her hands, Pandora looked away and choked out a

cry. Jackson's face immediately twisted with remorse. "But that doesn't matter anymore. I'm here now."
Jackson loved children, but he also loved Pandora. He was angry that she'd keep such a secret from him, and questioned if his heart would've loved her the same if he knew they would never really be a family.
Pandora stood before him, lifeless. Her emotions were becoming a monster about to swallow her whole. She knew the day would come when her past would come back to destroy her, and here it was. She tried to control what parts of herself she wanted Jackson to fall in love with. She never wanted him to see that she'd been broken from birth and came with a past that left her sick and twisted in ways he'd probably never understand. Beauty and the Beast for the masses- *a clever-cover up.* She also thought she could control her heart, but that too began to show its true colors. It was beating for Jackson but begging for Bruce and there was nothing she could do about it. Life was beginning to demand the truth from her, and she wasn't sure if she was prepared to face it all. Tears ripped through her eyes and cascaded down her face. She felt embarrassed, exposed, and weak.
Jackson watched the woman he loved crumble to ashes right in front of his face. He'd never seen her in this kind of state. It was like a veil had been ripped from his eyes and finally, he could see her for who she really was. He reached for her, but she backed away and rushed through the bedroom door to get out of her house.
"Anna, don't run," he called from the hallway. "We have to talk abou-." The front door slammed.

...An hour later

Pandora sat on top of Quinn's overstuffed teddy bear on the floor of her bedroom playing with Heaven. A dozen needles danced their way across her forehead, and an unsettling feeling churned in the pit of her stomach. She felt dense and detached from reality. She had no idea what her world was coming too, but she refused to stick around her house to find out. She needed an escape from herself and reality. The safest place on earth where she could be understood, unjudged, and loved for who she was, was with her friends.

Pandora giggled as Heaven wrapped her tiny arms around her neck, slobbering her with kisses and hysterical laughter. Listening to her innocent baby babble was the most beautiful sound in the world to Pandora. She wished she could go back to the days when life was that simple.

"Hey you two," Quinn entered her bedroom in her robe carrying a plate of chocolate chip cookies.

"Hey," Pandora laughed, preoccupied with Heaven.

"So, what happened?" Quinn sat down on the floor next to them.

"What do you mean?"

"I mean, what's gone wrong?"

"There has to be something wrong for me to come to visit my goddaughter?" Pandora reached for a cookie.

"No, that part is fine. Your sweatpants are on backward, your shirt is on inside out, and your sneakers are on the wrong feet, is what gave you away," Quinn laughed.

Pandora froze with the cookie in her mouth. She looked down at her attire and shook her head. Had her mind really been that discombobulated?

"I just needed to get away, that's all. Jackson and I had a fight about kids. I finally told him the truth."

"Oh no."

"Yeah, and his response bordered along the lines of, *"Gee, I wish I'd known this before I married you."*

Quinn's mouth fell open. "Exactly. And then there's Br-" She bit her lip, deciding to leave that piece of information out for now.

"There's what?"

"Nothing. Do you and Andre ever come out of your perfect bubble and get angry and argue like normal people?" Pandora asked, sarcastically.

"Of course we do," Quinn replied, amused.

"So, what do you do when you get angry? How do you channel it? Do you stay and fight it out, or do you run, like me?"

"Time. Tone. Turf."

"What?" Pandora raised an eyebrow.

"I watch my time. No serious conversations on Saturday, Sunday, or Tuesday. I make sure I say what I need to say using the right tone. I'm also mindful of turf,"

Quinn winked, "There are certain conversations I leave out of the bedroom. Some we have in public, or a neutral territory like dinner maybe, or the mall."

"Wait, so you guys have scheduled days to argue?" Pandora laughed.

"Yes," Quinn laughed back, "Certain days are just off-limits. It'll throw everything off. Saturdays, we get ready for Sunday, Sunday, we're too tired, and Tuesday is my biggest workday."

"That's actually pretty genius. Many of our arguments end up escalating because they happen during a time when one of us is exhausted or overwhelmed with work and other things. Like tonight."

"Exactly," Quinn nodded, "but then, there are days when we do get into it, and I don't feel like fighting fair. When that happens, I exit stage left and tell him when I'm ready to revisit the situation."

"What about yelling? I can't stand yelling and screaming. Jackson does that all the time when he's upset," Pandora cringed.

"Oh, I don't tolerate yelling. I speak and hear well. We're both gifted in the area of communication, so he can say what he needs to say to me in a modest tone."

"You know what? You remind me of all those exceptional women in the Bible that I try to learn from-but can't," Pandora looked at Quinn and chuckled, taking in her innocent aura. "I always have trouble learning from women who get it all right. Throughout my marriage, I've watched you. I've tried to model your good girl ways and it just doesn't work for me. I've spent my energy comparing, falling short, and asking myself how the hell do you do it," she laughed, "it's so discouraging."

"That's not true. I struggle every day just like anyone else. I've also been married for almost eleven years to a man I've been with for almost twenty years," Quinn replied, "so you can't expect to attain my kind of results in your second year of marriage."

"Shoot, I don't think I'll ever attain it. Sometimes when I try to read my Bible for inspiration I just shake my head, because I stumble upon women like Ruth who was extremely faithful, or Ester, who was courageous, and Mary, who was innocent. And then there's me, who's *so* none of the above."

"That's not true."

"It is. And then one day I happened upon Jezebel, and a bell went off," Pandora admitted, causing Quinn to burst into laughter. "Seriously, I could relate with her pushy personality, I understood her controlling ways, and I empathized with her angry outbursts."

"Right, and I'm sure you were aghast when you got to her gruesome ending. She's certainly someone that can teach you what *not* to do in your marriage."

"Sort of. But for the most part, she was in control of things. That *used* to be me. Now, everything is spiraling out of my control, and—"

"And nothing is working out for you, and God is sitting back saying, *good.* "

"Wow, that was *mean*," Pandora raised an eyebrow.

"Honey, I've been there before. I think God is trying to tell you to let go, be real with yourself *and* your emotions, and accept what he allows from it." Pandora thought deeply about Quinn's words.

"Besides, control never really guarantees you the life you want, nor does it guarantee the outcomes you think you need. I remember trying to create heaven on earth, but all I really created was hell on earth for me and everything connected to me. Once I stopped and just kept it real with myself, life got so much better."

"Maybe…" Pandora sighed.

"Try it…And if that doesn't work, we can always take a vacation and get away."

"Oh, speaking of vacation," her eyes lit up, "I have a lawyers retreat in D.C next weekend. Jackson can't go, he'll be away. How about you and Eden come with me?"

"Did somebody say vacation?" Eden slid into Quinn's room holding a cup of ice cream, "If so, count me all the way in."

"Hey," Pandora looked surprised, "I didn't know you were here. I thought you'd be enjoying your new home."

"*Please*," Quinn looked annoyed, "that was a waste of our money. She hasn't spent one night in that house."

"What? Why not?"

"I just like hanging out with Heaven, that's all," Eden lied. "She's so much more fun than being home." Eden jumped on the bed and crawled to the edge so she could be closer to Quinn and Pandora.

"What about Jade?" Quinn asked.

'What about her?"

"You two have such a great friendship. At least, that's what I thought. She told me you haven't said two words to her."

"Do you not like her anymore?" Pandora squinted, sensing something was wrong.

"I didn't say that."

"So why are you up under Quinn like you're afraid to go home?" Pandora folded her arms.

"No one's afraid," Eden quickly shot back.

"Then what's the problem? You complained about not having a home, and we got you one. You seemed so happy at first, an—"

"Pandora, will you just l*eave* it alone," Eden bit. Something about the sound of her voice and the fear in her eyes set off all kinds of alarms in Pandora's mind. Bruce was right. *Something wasn't adding up.* Eden got up off the bed and stormed out of the room. Quinn turned to look at Pandora.

"What was that all about?"

"That Jade," Pandora tapped her fingers on her leg, "I don't like that girl."

"Why doesn't anyone like her anymore?" Quinn asked, feeling completely out of the loop.

"I don't like her energy, and she's sneaky. I didn't trust her from day one. I'm only nice to her because you asked me for a favor."

"I just spoke to her this afternoon, and she told me you were the devil reincarnated."

"I've been a well-behaved devil, considering my feelings about her," Pandora pursed her lips. "I brought in Dwayne earlier today to meet her. He's on the board for the medical school she'll be interviewing for, and she made an inappropriate sexual pass at him right in front of my face."

"Dwayne?" Quinn gave Pandora the eye.

"*Dwayne*," Pandora returned the gesture. "I warned her to keep it professional and she got way beside herself. I also caught her snooping around my office."

"What?" Quinn clutched her chest, "I'm pretty good at reading people, and she didn't strike me as sneaky. Her spirit is so genuine around me."

"I think she's playing you," Pandora shook her head, "If she's so genuine, how come Eden won't go anywhere near her?" Quinn stared at Pandora with a puzzled look on her face. "Also," she lowered her voice, "Bruce looked deeper into Eden's relationship with Travis, and some of the things he discovered were really bothersome. At first, I just thought maybe he was being a bit fanatical, but something about the way Eden is acting is leading me to believe he's right."

"Right about what?"

"Travis may have been paid to kill Eden. He has a history of being a hitman, and there was money being sent from unknown accounts during the time him and Eden dated, but after Travis was killed, someone swiped the entire thing."

"What?" Quinn's high-pitched voice filled the room.

"Quinn!" Pandora hissed in a whisper, "Keep this to yourself for now. Bruce is gonna dig deeper into everything and see what he comes up with, and I'm gonna be working with him. I was hesitant about it all, but...I don't like how she's acting. She knows something, she's hiding from something, and she's afraid of something- her reason for not wanting to be home."

"But who would set Eden up? She hasn't done anything to anybody," Quinn replied, still trying to come to an understanding in her mind.

"I have no idea, but it's worrisome because Travis was killed, and Eden wasn't. Meaning, whoever they are, they could be trying to finish what he started." Quinn's eyes nearly distended from their sockets. Suddenly, Eden sticking close to her began to make sense.

"Oh my goodness…thankfully Travis had a bad aim." Pandora's eyes filled with anger. "Wait until I get my hands on whoever is behind this. I'm gonna put a bullet straight through *their* head. And my aim is *perfect.*"

Chapter 9

Rebound

"Explain this to me again?" Pandora asked, finding it difficult to wrap her head around Bruce's plan as she sat in his office two days later.

"Savanna has to do a workshop at the convention, and she wants me there for it. She also has to leave two days earlier, but I can't because I'm stuck here for work. I wanted to ride with you," Bruce sat down at his desk.

"I don't have enough room. My car is full already." Pandora's mind had been flooded with thoughts of Bruce for the last two days. The last thing she wanted to do was be trapped in a car with him for four hours.

"With who? Eden and Quinn? You have that roomy Aston Martin, there's plenty of room for one more. I can squeeze in. I'm not that big," he joked.

"Bruce?" she sighed, "Wouldn't your fiancée pitch a fit if she knew me- your *ex*-girlfriend, picked you up from the house you two shared and did her the favor of driving you to a convention; *With two other women in the car*."

Bruce took a moment to consider the question but didn't understand.

"Why would she have a fit? We're all college friends." Pandora's heart did a bungee jump into her stomach. *Is that how he defined them*?

"Listen, I think me coming to your house and allowing you into my car is a really, *really* bad idea," Pandora replied softly, out of excuses. Bruce held her stare for a moment, then lowered his chin.

"So you're gonna leave me high and dry?" He looked at her, defeated, and there it was. The part of her that really *was* his friend wanted to do him a favor. She had an overwhelming desire to wrap her arms around Bruce and tell him "sure, you can come with us," just to see his beautiful smile again.

"I know I'm asking a huge favor. I know you're married. I know I'm engaged, and I get that you wanna be professional. I'm asking because this is a really big deal for me. I don't want to miss Savanna's workshop, and I also don't want to miss the meetings lined up for this next case I'm on," his voice scratched, "Come on, Anna. I *need* you." Three words. The ones he only *really* needed to say...

"Alright," Pandora crossed her arms, "I'll be there to get you at 10 am." Bruce's eyebrows shot up, and his lips tilted into that smile she loved so much.

"You're the best! I owe you."

"You're paying for gas," she rolled her eyes.

"That's fine."

"And tolls."

"I'll pay for lunch too," he promised. Dressed in a well-fitted black suit that almost looked tapered to his body, Bruce winked and got up from his desk. The white shirt he wore underneath was left unbuttoned, revealing some of the definition in his body. "So, what's up?" He waited for Pandora to answer, but she seemed star-struck and lost in her thoughts by the sight of him. His gaze slid over hers. Pandora was his joy and the light of his dark world. He would've done anything to make sure she was carefree and content for the rest of her life. Even if that meant respecting her boundaries and doing the unthinkable; remaining professional and *leaving her alone.*

"What?" It took her a minute to snap out of her thoughts and register what Bruce was saying.

"You said you had some new information about Eden."

"Oh, that's right," she remembered, "I spoke to her briefly yesterday, and I totally agree that something is up. She had that look on her face like she was hiding something, but won't say what it is.

"Well bring her in for questioning."

"No," she shook her head, "I don't want her anywhere near this. She's obviously afraid of something, otherwise she would have said something already. If she's been set up, that means they're watching her and watching us. I feel like she's protecting herself by keeping quiet."

"I don't think that's a good idea. What if he, she...or they have already gotten to her and are threatening her to stay quiet?"

"I doubt it," Pandora shook her head, "her energy would be totally different if she were being threatened. She would've found a way to let us know. She's been up under Quinn and refuses to stay in the house we bought for her to share with her girlfriend. Speaking of which, find out *everything* you can about her.

"The roommate?"

"Yes, her name is Jade," she fumbled for a last name, "Jade Harris. She's an intern in my office and there's something about her I don't like. From my knowledge, Eden met Travis through *her*." Bruce jotted down information on his computer.

"Got it. I've been doing my own digging, too. I went so far back as to looking into Miss Ruby's death. I find it hard to believe Ruby was just in the wrong place at the wrong time," Bruce said.

The woman who shot her, Ashley Peterson-"

"I worked the case that put her in jail," Pandora admitted.

"Yeah, I remember. So why didn't she come after *you*? What would it benefit her to come after your best friend's mother?" Bruce narrowed his eyes as Pandora stood silently trying to put pieces together in her own head.

"Are there any other persons of interest I should be worried about? I have records that show Eden was also pregnant and lost a baby. Do you know the father?"

Wide-eyed and embarrassed, Pandora swallowed and crossed her arms.

"Yeah...he's my...*he's my husband*."

Bruce's eyes flew open at her statement.

"I'm sorry*, what*?"

"Why is this even important?" Pandora huffed, "We're talking about Eden and a possible criminal. My husband, her baby, Miss Ruby- this is all way in left field."

"Listen," Bruce looked up, "I don't care to involve myself in your drama. My job is to look at all the facts, so that's what I'm doing."

Pandora sighed.

"Eden and I unknowingly dated the same guy for a couple of years, and she was pregnant by him, but lost the baby at eight months."

"Eight months," Bruce dropped his pen and reared his head back, "Were there any health issues?"

"No," Pandora shrugged, "the doctors said her blood pressure spiked out of control and her body temporarily threw itself out of whack." Bruce looked at Pandora and squinted. Something about that story didn't fit right *either*.

"Who is this guy? How did you two meet?" Pandora took a deep breath and turned her gaze in a different direction. Softly closing her eyes, she shook her head, remembering the fateful day she had her first run-in with Jackson.

Virginia, Four years ago….

It was just shy of 7 am and Pandora lay scatterbrained in Bruce's California king-sized bed, wrapped in his arms while they rested peacefully in the home he shared with his wife and daughter. She'd been preparing herself all week to defend a woman named Ashley Peterson who was on trial for capital murder, and the day of the trial had finally come. She'd barely slept all night thinking about it. Throughout Pandora's career, she made a name for herself defending the lives of rapists, assassins, drug lords, child molesters, and serial killers, but this was the first time she'd be defending someone on trial for the death penalty. Knowing that someone else's fate lay in her hands made her extremely nervous, but thankfully, she had Bruce to keep her mind off of things.

After their lustful re-acquaintance at the lawyer's convention eight years ago, Bruce and Pandora had been tied at the hip just like old times. If it weren't for the ring on his finger, you would've never thought he was married with a family. He and Pandora were best friends, confidants, lovers, teachers, listeners, and critics to one another. Bruce found loopholes and made ways to spend every Christmas, Valentines', and birthday with Pandora. They traveled the world together and committed themselves to being the best that two people could find and bring out in one another.

Bruce's wife, Angela, understood that being a detective called for him to lead a very busy life, so she never grew skeptical of his disappearing acts. If she only knew just how busy he actually was. Bruce and Pandora accented each other beautifully. The love they shared deepened and enriched every facet of their lives. Their happiness was fuller, their memories were fresher, and their commitment was stronger. They had a kindred connection deeper than every broken vow Bruce recited to Angela on their wedding day. He often felt terrible living a double life because it caused him to miss out on so many of his daughter's milestones. His only child, Sasha, was his pride and joy, and the sole reason he chose to remain trapped in a loveless marriage.

For years, the thought of divorcing Angela to be with Pandora weighed heavily on his mind, but Sasha was the silver lining for him to stick around. She was the focus for every reason to deal with his unhappiness, lack of sex, and conversations that only revolved around household duties. At nine years old, Sasha was extremely intelligent and aware of everything. She was daddy's princess and looked at him like he was her hero. The last thing Bruce wanted was for her to look at him as the bad guy; the daddy who left her and her mother high and dry to start another family. He also knew that leaving his family to be with another woman involved more risks than just losing his daughter. It could ruin both his and Pandora's career and reputation. Pandora would be labeled as "the other woman," which would carry just as much, if not more of a negative stigma than him being known as the adulterous husband. They both would lose friends and family support, and he cringed at the thought of doing that to her. He was torn between wanting to be a good father and wanting to stop hiding what his heart truly desired since middle school. He had no idea what to do, so he left it alone and learned to live in the moment.

"Wake up," Pandora tapped on his Herculean chest, "It's 7:15, I have to go soon." At the sound of her voice, Bruce's eyes slowly opened.

"I have to get up, too," he murmured, "I have to get to the airport by 9."

"Alright, let's get a move on then."

An hour later they had both dressed, eaten breakfast and Pandora was out the back door in her car.

"Good luck with your case. Call me as soon as you're done, okay?"

"I will," she nodded, "Good luck in Florida."

"I'll be back first thing Friday morning. I'm gonna miss you like crazy."

"I know," she pouted, "are you sure you don't want me to meet you there? Once this case is over, I'm taking a month-long hiatus to mentally recover. Palm trees and the Florida sun sound like a wonderful place to do it.

"Baby, I'll literally be in meetings from sun up to sundown. I don't want you waiting around in some hotel or venturing off alone. As soon as I get back, we'll take a trip somewhere to refresh," he promised.

"Okay," she glanced at her clock on the dashboard, "I have to go, see you soon."

"I love you," he planted a kiss on her forehead and backed away from her car. "I see you're wearing my necklace. It looks amazing around your neck."

"Boy, I've been wearing this necklace for the last four years every time I work a high profile case," she laughed, touching the canary yellow diamond-encrusted necklace he'd bought for her.

"That's why you win every time. You have me by your side," he winked, as Pandora laughed at his corny humor and sped off. Bruce watched her car disappear from the block and almost immediately, he wished she was back in his arms. Since he was old enough to understand what love was, wanting Pandora never stopped. Turning around, he walked back into his house and retreated back into his bedroom to take the sheets off his bed and throw them into the washing machine. An hour later he'd packed his bag, and was making his way to the garage when Sasha came bolting through the front door.

"Daddy!"

"Hey!" Bruce looked at his watch, "what are you doing here? You're supposed to be in school."

"Whatever," she laughed, "Mommy already told me we were going to Disney World!" Angela walked into the house laughing.

"I didn't tell her anything. She saw the plane tickets in the glove compartment." Bruce laughed as Angela walked into him with a kiss.

"Well now that the secret is out, let's get going. We have to be at the airport in forty-five minutes!"

...45 minutes later

Pandora drove down the highway en route to her office to go over some final notes before heading to court. She smiled to herself as she twitched in her Mercedes, still feeling the effects of Bruce from earlier. The love they made was always passionate and amazing, leaving her on cloud nine. This was the first time in eight years that he'd traveled out of state without her, and although she'd miss him she knew she didn't have time to get stuck in her girly emotions. She had a big case in less than two hours and needed to be mentally prepared. Just as she began going over her opening remarks in her head, her cellphone rang.

"Joanna'" she answered.

"Anna, baby, good morning. Where are you right now?" Miss Ruby's urgent voice bellowed through the phone.

"Hi, Miss. Ruby, I'm on my way to the office, and then court. How's Hawaii?"

"I wouldn't know," she said, annoyed, "My plane just touched back down in Virginia. I left Eden to run the salon while I was gone, and of course, I don't know what the hell I was thinking. The fool didn't lock up properly and my store got robbed."

"What?" Pandora gasped, "When?"

"Last night, so I caught an early flight back to town. If it's not too much trouble, can you pick me up from the airport?"

"Sure," Pandora quickly drove into the left lane, and made a U-turn toward the airport, "I'll be there in ten minutes."

"Thanks so much. I'll be at baggage claim B. I tried calling Eden, but she's not answering."

"I spoke to her yesterday. I wonder why she didn't let me know the shop got robbed."

"Because she's embarrassed and feels responsible. If you happen to get a hold of her before you get to me, you let her know I'm gonna beat the black off of her with the padlock she forgot to attach to my salon door!" A dial tone signaled in Pandora's ear as she put the phone down and laughed out loud. Ten minutes later she pulled up in front of the Virginia airport and double-parked along the front. Getting out of her car, she grabbed her cellphone to dial Ruby's number, when a familiar female voice sounded in her ear.

"Oh my goodness, Joanna!" Pandora turned around to see Angela rushing over to her.

"Hi," Pandora jerked her head back, taken by surprise. It was a bit shocking and uncomfortable coming face to face with a woman whose husband she'd been sleeping with for almost a decade.

"I haven't seen you in years! How have you been?"

"I've been wonderful," Pandora extended a half-smile, "How's the law firm treating you?"

"Certainly not as good as yours. Our team is still only handling low profile cases. I'm trying to make partner, but I haven't had any luck thus far."

"I remember those days. Stick with it. It'll happen."

"Oh absolutely. I steal pointers and tips from your firm's website all the time. You have that big Peterson case this morning, don't you?" Angela looked at her watch.

"I do. I'm actually just here picking up a friend."

"Well good luck, you'll need it. I'm headed to Disney with Bruce and Sasha. He took the whole week off to treat us to a vacation," she cheesed in excitement, "this is Sasha's first time, so of course, she's been flipping out ever since she found out." Pandora's caramel complexion nearly went pale. "Honey, come over here! Look who I just ran into," Angela motioned for Bruce to come join them.

"Sweetheart, I'm in lin-" Bruce turned around and froze when he saw Pandora. It was almost as if his soul had jumped right out of his body.

"It's so crazy; I knew you had this case coming up since it's been all over the news. I asked my husband last week if he'd heard from you and he told me he couldn't even remember the last time he'd spoken to you. What a coincidence! Looks like we spoke you into fruition."

Coincidence was right. Last week, Pandora had Bruce pinned to the mirror of Angela's makeup closet slow grinding his brains out. It's no wonder he had a foggy memory.

"Yeah," Pandora blinked, trying to ward off the shock, "It's been a really busy few years for me."

"Hey, Anna," Bruce nervously scratched his neck.

"Hello, detective," she bit with a coldness, folding her arms across her stomach. "You guys have fun in Florida, I should get going."

"What a beautiful necklace!" Angela gasped, "Look, baby, doesn't that look like the one you gave me for our anniversary five years ago? The one I lost somewhere in the house and never found," she shook her head and laughed. "I'm such a klutz." Pandora openly stared back at Bruce. It took everything in her not to rip that necklace off and choke him to death. Bruce's mouth slacked, gazing back at Pandora with a face full of guilt and regret.

"Sweetheart, Sasha's been in the bathroom for a while now, why don't you go see what's taking her so long," he requested, but it sounded more like a plea.

"She certainly has. I'll go check now. Anna, good luck today, it was nice seeing you." Angela smiled, quickly walking off. Pandora stood lifeless in front of Bruce. It felt as if the magic carpet she'd been on for the last eight years had been snatched from under her feet. Her air supply seemed to get less and less and it felt like the airport ceiling would come crashing down on her at any minute.

"Ann-"

"There you are," Ruby walked up and slid her arm under Pandora's, in just the right time too, because she didn't know how much more strength her legs had before they gave away. "I called you fifty times."

"I'm…I'm sorry," she struggled to find her voice, "Are you ready? I'm running a little behind schedule."

"I'm ready when you are," Ruby noticed Bruce staring back at them like a deer in headlights.

"Oh my goodness, it's Bruce. Hi Bruce!"

"Hi," he replied, his voice barely audible.

"How are yo-" Ruby's words were cut off by Pandora urging her toward the exit.

"He's actually running late for a flight, and I'm running late for court."

"Oh. Have fun," she waved with a smile. Bruce wanted so badly to chase after Pandora, but he knew it wouldn't have mattered at this point.

"Thanks so much for coming to pick me up, honey. You're a lifesaver." They exited the airport and walked toward her car. Ruby walked ahead to place her bag in the trunk just as Pandora turned toward a nearby trashcan. Her stomach had twisted into knots of anxiety until she was nauseous and ready to throw up. Leaning over, she hurled out the bagel and cappuccino Bruce had made for her earlier.

"Anna," Ruby rushed over and patted her back, "Are you okay?" Pandora nodded and coughed into the trashcan. Ruby handed her a paper towel and she wiped her mouth and discarded it.

"I'm fine. It's just my nerves."

"My goodness," Ruby winced. She turned around and walked toward the car. Pandora quickly snatched off the necklace and tossed it into the vomit filled trashcan.

Her hands shook and tears started to fall from her eyes. She wanted to scream bloody murder and commit it too.

She'd been lied too and gaslighted by the only man she
ever loved. How could he? Suddenly she realized she'd
been living in a fantasy world for the last eight years, and
reality had finally slapped her in the face. It didn't matter
how much history she had with Bruce, he was married
and didn't belong to her. He was having an affair with
another woman. *She* was the other woman. Pandora had
to almost drag her legs to her car and force her body into
the driver's seat. Ruby raised an eyebrow at her but kept
quiet.

"Just drop me off wherever you're going. I can get Eden
to pick me up from there."

"Sure," Pandora shook herself out of entropy, started the
car, and pulled off. "So tell me again what happened with
the salon?"

Ruby began going into a rant about what happened, but
all Pandora could hear was a ringing in her ears. What
had she done to herself? Never in her life did she imagine
being in a relationship that had a glass ceiling, yet here
she was caught in a love triangle, stuck in something that
would never grow. She'd been building a life with Bruce
that would never amount to anything other than being
second best. Once upon a time, they had real love, and
Pandora allowed Bruce to convince her that they were
rebuilding it. When she thought about it now, however,
all that had been built was sneaking around, good sex,
and false hope.

In the beginning stages of their affair, Pandora told
herself that she was better off dating a married man. In
the past, whenever she and Bruce had gotten back
together after a breakup, life found a way to once again

tear them to pieces. Her heart was tired of it, so she learned to take from him what she could get. Sustaining a relationship where Bruce was ultimately unavailable would prevent them both from being truly intimate and emotionally close. She told herself that doing so would prevent her from feeling the pain of heartbreak in that deep, core cutting way she'd felt so many times before. In return, she got good sex, lavish vacations, and eight years of a perpetual first date. But now she realized she was a fool. Seeing Bruce with his wife and realizing she had allowed herself to be played left a huge hole in her heart. She would've rather died than feel what she felt in that moment. Throughout her career, Pandora had met so many women who had gone through the same thing and she promised herself it would never be her. Those women thrived off of having friends with benefits and it ruined them. Her lawyer friends casually slept around with married men, promising never to get attached, but they always failed. Pandora watched as careers were severed and friendships never recovered because boundaries were breached. A fierce determination overcame Pandora in the car. Despite playing into the dirty game of love, she swore to herself that the game was officially over. Words couldn't describe how much she loved Bruce, but he didn't belong to her. She didn't need that kind of distraction and didn't want that complication anymore. Her career was right where it was supposed to be, and come hell, high water, or orgasms that made her forget her social security number, she was determined that's where it would stay. *Simple.* But the sick feeling in her stomach, the tinge of sour jealousy on the tip of her tongue- there was nothing simple about that.

Pandora shook her head, warding off the onset of tears, determined to shake off the melancholy right along with it. "It doesn't matter how I feel," she coached herself in silence, "I am not one of those girls. I am not ruled by my emotions. Put it aside, Anna- like last season's Gucci bag." Pandora was so consumed in her thoughts, she didn't even feel her phone vibrating in her pocket. As she came to a traffic light, she pulled it out and glanced at it. "I filed for divorce last week. Florida is where I planned to give her the papers and talk about where to go from here. I lived a lie for so long for the sake of my daughter, but I can't do it anymore. You're who I want. You're who I need."

Another text flashed across the screen, "I'm sorry about the necklace. I purchased it for you, but she found it, so I gave it to her as an anniversary gift, and-"

Refusing to read any more of the text, Pandora snatched the phone out of her view and tossed it out of the window. As she drove through the light, her mind wandered.

"I don't wanna hear that B.S. But, is he really filing for divorce? Maybe I'm overreacting. Maybe he does- *No*. Objection. Out of order. Cease and desist. We all know what happens when you play with matches—but I will not get burned a second time. I'm fireproof. The *hell* with him."

 After finally leaving Ruby, getting to court, and periodically going into the bathroom to cry her eyes out over Bruce, Pandora lost her first case, ever. Ashley was sentenced to death, and Pandora had embarrassed herself on national television. She forgot most of her speech and stuttered through her arguments, but it hadn't hit her yet. Visions of everything that happened with Bruce still danced in her mind. She needed to get rid of those thoughts, and she needed to get rid of him. For good. Once court was over, Pandora rushed back into the bathroom, closed the door, and spun around with her body pressed against the doorframe. She let out a sigh as she closed her eyes and envisioned the way one of the jurors had been undressing her with his eyes the whole time. Normally, she paid no attention to it. But today, it was time for a change.

"Thinking about me?" Said a deep baritone voice in the restroom. Pandora popped her eyes open just in time to see Jackson's six foot six chiseled body standing in front of her. *Hell.* Maybe she was.

"We met in court one day," Pandora said coldly, getting up from her seat. Listen, I really have to get going. Let me know what your further research comes up with.

"Will do," Bruce watched her shuffle for her belongings. Pandora bolted through his office door and down the emergency exit. Her feet took her all the way to the first floor before they gave away and she slammed herself into the wall and burst into tears.

Chapter 10

Caught up

Pandora, Eden, and Quinn drove along the outskirts of Virginia in Pandora's black Aston Martin en route to pick up Bruce.

"It feels *so* good to get away," Eden sat in the front seat, relaxing her feet on Pandora's window sill.

"Tell me about it," Quinn sighed, "Remember the days we used to travel every month?"

"Remember this?" Pandora snickered. Reaching into her glove compartment, she pulled out a can of orange spray paint disguised in a can of Vidal Sassoon hair spray.

"Oh my goodness, you still have that?" Quinn laughed. "That's the spray paint she used in Abu Dhabi to vandalize those camels after the owner called us monkeys?"

"And Mexico when she destroyed the hotel room after the snobby hotel director charged her credit card an extra five hundred dollars for a broken lamp."

"Five hundred dollars for that cheap, dollar store lamp," Pandora sneered in disgust, as they all shared a laugh. "Eden, how's the shop coming along? Are you handling it well?"

"It's alright I guess. Definitely not something I would create a career out of. I don't see how my mom dealt with all of those opinionated, picky people. No one seems to be satisfied. Like, *ever*."

"Regardless, I'm so proud of you," Pandora gleamed, "You've come such a long way in the last year."

"No honey, *you're* the one deserving a round of applause," Eden replied.

"Why?"

"Because we're headed to Bruce's house, and your smiling, happy, and in good spirits."

"Oh no, *here we go*. I knew it was coming."

"Well, I was going to mind my business and go with the flow," Quinn said, "but since Eden bought it up, I have questions."

"So do I."

"And I don't have any answers that I haven't already given you," Pandora sighed,

"He asked me for a ride and I said yes. *That's it.*"

"A few weeks ago she told us they were cordial associates. Now, we're driving to his house and giving him rides like a taxi," Eden rolled her eyes.

"Mmhmm...I wish she'd just tell us the truth," Quinn muttered back.

"That is the truth!" Pandora hissed, pulling into Bruce's driveway. Eden and Quinn tilted forward and pursed their lips at her. "Oh my goodness, whatever. Next topic, please."

After the meltdown she had last week, Pandora had no peace in her mind or in her house. She and Jackson were at each other's throats, and she could barely concentrate on work because her mind was so wrapped up in Bruce. Finally, she took Quinn's advice and let everything go.

Pandora was a good wife, and deep down she knew that keeping a secret from her husband for the last two years was wrong, so she swallowed her pride and gave him an honest apology and prayed they could work through it. While Jackson was still upset, he was ready to stop the fighting and move forward. They could work through it, Jackson agreed, and all was well in the Ford household. Pandora also accepted that she may never fully get over Bruce. She couldn't control her heart. Every time she tried, things always ended in bloodshed. Bruce took up space and emotions in her mind that was wreaking havoc over her life that she didn't need. She cried in the shower every night, begging God to make her stop loving him so she could finally move on. She knew God wasn't a microwave God and that things would take time, so she moved on with her life as best as she could while she waited.

However, the second Bruce emerged from his house, all of that wait on the Lord stuff went up in smoke. Bruce was dressed in a white tank top, distressed jean shorts, and a white baseball cap. The muscles in his arms and legs moved in tune to his stride. The sun had transformed his already dark complexion into a rough, deep shade of mahogany; a black coffee with no cream. As he made his way down the steps, Eden moved her feet from the ledge of the car and leaned forward to get a better view. Quinn sat in the back and tilted her glasses, gawking at him through the tinted window.

"Hey, ladies," Bruce's dazzling smile revealed the bronze glow under his cheeks.

"Hey Detective," Quinn and Eden replied in unison.

"He looks like walking artwork," Quinn mumbled under her breath.

"Good luck trying to pretend like you don't see *that* this weekend," Eden looked at Pandora and smirked. Pandora blinked her eyes and played it cool as the three of them exited the car.

"Long time no see," Bruce gave Quinn a hug.

"Tell me about it. It's been what, five years now?"

"I know. I've gotta get over there to see my boy, Andre. I heard you two have a baby and everything now, that's awesome." He moved along to Eden, "And *you*. What's up, soldier? Come here!"

"Hey Bruce," Eden cheesed. He dropped his bag and scooped Eden into his arms, lifting her off her feet.

"I'm so happy to see you alive and well. How are you feeling?" He squeezed her tight and planted a kiss on her cheek.

"I feel great, thanks." Bruce cut his eyes at Pandora and smirked, reaching out to hug her.

"Hey you,"

"Hey back at you, honey," Pandora embraced him, hoping he couldn't feel her racing heart.

"What? I've upgraded to *honey* now?" He clutched his chest, "Be still my heart. She's friendly after all."

"Don't push it," Pandora warned with a laugh, popping open the trunk of her car.

"What in the world?" He gawked, widely staring at all of the luggage in the trunk. "Are you blind? You're driving an Aston Martin, not a Winnebago." Pandora took off her sunglasses. Her eyes clouded with genuine confusion.

"Are you suggesting we over packed?"

"I'm suggesting you'll need to narrow it down and take what you need."

"What do you mean? We're women. We *need* all of it."

"Do you see what I packed?" He held up an old raggedy gym bag. "*This* is my luggage for two days."

"And we should change our packing habits because you choose to live like a hobo? Not gonna happen." Bruce shook his head and squeezed his Wal-Mart bag in between their Louis Vuitton's and Gucci luggage. Once the trunk had closed, Pandora walked around to the driver's side. She could feel Bruce's eyes on her and she wanted so badly to continue to look forward, but curiosity got the better of her. She was dressed in a sleeveless white jumpsuit that was loose, but elegant. A floppy white straw sunhat and a pair of big round sunglasses covered half her face. In the light of the early Virginia sun, she nearly took Bruce's breath away. She turned back to see his smoldering brown eyes gazing at her with a deep intensity.

"You see something you like, Detective?"

"Yeah...that...that jumpsuit," he recovered, "my fiancée has it in black." Pandora pursed her lips with a smile and watched Bruce walk to the passenger seat with a cock-sure grin on his face. *This was going to be a long ride.*

Four hours later, they were all inside the crowded Hilton hotel. Eden and Quinn waited by a fountain watching the many lawyers coming in and out while Pandora checked them in at the front desk. Bruce walked back and forth from Pandora's car, putting all of their bags onto the hotel cart.

"Anna, what's your room number so I can take your bags up?"

"We're room 4320," Pandora turned around and handed Bruce a room key.

"Is that everything from the car?" Quinn asked as she and Eden walked over to join them.

"Just mine is left. All ten of your bags are accounted for," Bruce grimaced.

"*Well I have plenty* of bags in my trunk that need to be brought up," an attitude laced voice sounded behind them. They all turned to see Bruce's fiancée, Savanna standing there with a smug grin on her face.

"Hey, baby," Bruce smiled, surprised.

"Hello there, stud," she walked into his arms and planted an erotic kiss on Bruce's lips, making sure Quinn, Eden, and Pandora were in full view of it.

"Baby, these are my friends. This is Mannequin, Eden, and Anna. Anna's a lawyer at the Jenkins firm. The four of us grew up together," he proclaimed proudly.

"Hello, nice to meet you Savanna," Quinn smiled gracefully, extending her hand out.

Savanna gave all three ladies a brief once over before flickers of jealousy began to surface in her eyes. Savanna was five foot five, one hundred and fifteen pounds. She had smooth mocha skin and brown back length hair that was pulled back into a bun. She was a pretty woman but knew she had nothing on the impeccable beauty that drove down with her husband-to-be. She wasn't too fond of that at all. Savanna looked at Quinn's hand and crossed her arms with a head nod.

"It's a pleasure." Raising an eyebrow, Quinn blinked and took her hand away. Eden winced, and Pandora parted her lips at Savanna's blunt ignorance. "Anyway, sweetheart, you missed my morning presentation. I thought you said you'd be here by 11."

"I thought we would, I'm sorry," Bruce replied, "We got hungry and stopped to grab a bite to eat. Traffic was a bit hectic as well, so we ended up taking the scenic route."

"And you couldn't call or text to let me know this?" Savanna looked at him, annoyed.

"It totally slipped my mind baby, I apologize." He reached down to kiss her forehead. Pandora was instantly annoyed.

"I did *so* well earlier, too. Maybe next time your little *friend*s here will stick to the schedule.

"Whoa," Quinn winced.

"Excuse me?" Pandora tilted forward, making sure she heard correctly.

"Savanna?" Bruce furrowed, partly confused at her smart remark.

"Bruce, this was important to me. You said you'd be there and you weren't. On top of that, you didn't even bother to call me and let me know where you were."

"Well next time *take him with you*," Pandora hissed, "my car doesn't run off of anyone else's planned schedule."

"I'm sorry," Savanna looked Pandora up and down, confused, "Who are you again?"

"Savanna!" Bruce clutched her arm and pulled her to the side. Pandora's face turned crimson red. Eden and Quinn had to snatch her away before she lost her mind and acted like an idiot in front of all of her colleagues.

"Where in the world did he find *that* bimbo?" Eden gawked with a whisper.

"I don't know, but he'd better put her in her place before I do it!" Pandora threatened.

"Anna, relax," Quinn replied. "She seems jealous and insecure. That has nothing to do with us."

"I'll secure my foot up her *ass*. I don't-"

"Ladies, I'm *so sorry*," Bruce rushed over, wiping nervous beads of sweat from his brow, "Listen, she's just tense. It's my fault for not calling. She didn't mean to take it out on you guys."

"Right. And that's the woman you're vowing to spend the rest of your life with?" Pandora jerked her head back, "*God bless you.*"

"Alright, play nice," Bruce declared, offended. "She has another presentation in ten minutes so she needs her foundation and hairspray from my gym bag. I'll go-"

"No, *I'll* go- you go ahead and walk your dog and stay clear away from us this weekend."

"Anna, *come on*, give her a chance. You've had far worse moments-" Pandora rushed through the main lobby ahead of everyone and bolted through the exit doors before he could finish his sentence.

"I say we catch her in the bathroom," Eden rushed down the steps with Quinn as they followed Pandora to the car.

"No. It's not worth it," Quinn replied.

"She doesn't seem like someone Bruce would even associate with. It looks like he took her straight out of the ghetto and put Louboutin's on her," Eden laughed at herself.

"Stop it, Eden," Quinn chuckled.

"*It's true.* Did you see that rusty looking make-" Eden gasped through a giggle when she saw Pandora switching the hair spray in Bruce's gym bag with the orange spray paint in her glove compartment.

"Jo-*anna*," Quinn hissed, rushing to the car, "Don't you *dare*."

"Too late," Pandora dropped the decoy spray can in Bruce's bag and zipped it up.

"Oh my goodness, and it's the same Vidal Sassoon can," Eden covered her mouth, her wide eyes stared in amusement. Pandora strutted back toward the hotel lobby while Eden and Quinn trailed by her side.

"Can we stay for her presentation, *please?* I have to see this?" Eden laughed profusely.

"No. Anna take that spray paint out of that man's bag immediately." Quinn tried her best to snatch it but Pandora moved out of her reach. Bruce rushed to the lobby door and swung it open quickly. Savanna could be heard fussing all the way up the hall.

"She's on in two minutes. I need this," he reached for his gym bag.

"*Pandora*," Quinn threatened through clenched teeth.

"My pleasure," Pandora smiled, a hint of mischief tinted her brown eyes as she handed him his bag.

"I got the bellhop to take everyone's bags up. Can we meet up later for dinner so we can all talk? Please? I regret the way all of this happened. I could have prevented it..."

"*Not as regretful as she'll be*," Eden mumbled under her breath.

"Call us later," Pandora nearly walked through Bruce to get into the hotel lobby. "Maybe we'll answer. Maybe we won't." Bruce sighed. He felt terrible, but he was also on a schedule. Shaking his head, he rushed toward the bathroom to give Savanna her bag.

"So, who's ready for a fun-filled weekend?" Pandora smiled at her best friends.

"I feel like we just checked into the Bates Motel," Quinn cringed, disgusted.

"Let's go change and check out the spa. I've heard good reviews about it," Eden said.

"I'm not going anywhere within 100 feet of that meeting room where that woman is about to speak."

"Well, the spa is downstairs," Pandora giggled, sliding her arm under Quinn's. They all got on the elevator and made their way to their respective room. Twenty minutes later, they had changed into their bikinis and were fixing their hair in the mirror when Pandora's cell phone went off. She went over to look at it but walked away with a grin when she saw Bruce's name flashing on the screen. Quinn saw the look on her face and knew it was Bruce.

"Are you not gonna get that, Norma Bates?"

"Nope. He can leave a message. I'm busy." The phone rang on four more separate occasions and Pandora paid it no mind.

"Something has happened, and I want to know what it is," Eden said eagerly just as their room phone began to ring.

"Then you answer it," Pandora responded coldly. Eden walked over to the phone and answered on the third ring. "Hello?"

"Eden!" Bruce's angry voice echoed through their room.

"Hi Bruce," she responded politely, glancing back at Quinn and Pandora. Quinn clutched her chest in fear, and Pandora kept right on fixing her makeup.

"Where's Pandora?!"

"She's standing right here in the mirror. We're about to go -"

"Put her on the phone!" Bruce could hear a brief muffled talking before Eden's voice returned to the phone.

"She said she's busy and she'll call you back when she feels like it."

"Eden?" Bruce hissed, "Tell your friend I said to get on this got damn phone right the hell now before I come up there and beat her ass!" There was a shocked pause before Eden replied.

"You want me to tell her that?"

"Tell her *exactly* that!" His urgent furious voice yelled into the phone.

"Anna," Eden turned to face Pandora, enthused at what was about to go down, "Bruce said to get on this got damn phone right the hell now before he comes upstairs and beats your ass." Bruce could hear Pandora practically stomping to the phone, muttering all kinds of obscenities on the way.

"Have you *lost* your mind?" Pandora fussed into the phone, "Don't threaten me!"

"Joanna, *what the hell* am I looking at right now?!" He unleashed his fury. It obviously wasn't his best opener, but he found it hard to be logical when his fiancée stood in front of hundreds of law firms looking like carrot top.

"I don't know Bruce, what the hell *are* you looking at?" She shot back.

"Don't play with me! Is orange the new black?! Why does my fiancée look like a pumpkin!?"

"October *is* next month. Maybe she's prepping for an early Halloween." Bruce nearly jumped through the phone.

"This has your name written all over it. There are all types of important clients and prospects in that meeting. Do you have *any* idea how much you just ruined her career!"

"Stop yelling at me!" Pandora screeched.

"What is *wrong* with you!?"

"There's nothing wrong with *me*. She put her foot in her *own* mouth. I wonder how it tastes."

"You know what?" Bruce's deep voice bellowed into the phone. Pandora went to say something but a dial tone sounded in her ear.

"What happened?" Quinn asked, concerned.

"What do you think happened," Pandora slammed the phone down with an attitude, "he's throwing a tantrum over his fiancée's hair. Oh well. He's lucky it wasn't acid."

"I can't believe she just sprayed her hair without checking in a mirror," Eden shook her head.

"I can't believe Pandora had the guts to embarrass-" A loud banging on the door caused all three of them to jump.

"*Open* this door before I kick it in!" Bruce threatened from the outside.

"Oh my gosh, Anna he's gonna *kill* you," Eden dodged away from the door.

"*Please,*" she walked toward the door with a hand on her hip. "You have one more time to threaten m-" With one hard foot from his size 13 sneaker, Bruce kicked in the hotel door in with a force that nearly made the entire floor shake. The lock completely shattered and Bruce stood in the entrance like an angry lion. Quinn and Eden both jumped back to safety.

"You wrecked my marriage the first time, you will *not* do it again!" He barricaded through the opening, walking furiously toward her.

"*I* wrecked your marriage, are you serious!?" Pandora fussed back.

"Yes. Yes, you did! You tell everything else, but I highly doubt you told your friends *that.*"

"Bruce," Pandora laughed angrily, trying to calm herself down, "I suggest you get o-"

"I will get out when I'm done," he backed her into a wall, "after I tell everybody how I cheated on my wife for eight years chasing after you! How you slept in my bed more than she did!" Quinn and Eden's mouth dropped open. A flush swept across Pandora's cheeks as her nostrils flared. She was angry, but the guilt from her previous behavior slammed into her as well.

"Did I put a gun to your head and tell you to step out on your wife?"

"After everything I gave up for you, I wish you *would* have! I left my wife, I lost my daughter- she hates me. I did it all to be with you, and you played me for a *fool*. I came back for you and you disappeared and fell in love with somebody else," Bruce yelled at the top of his lungs. "I spent the last four years trying to get over you. I found somebody else and I'm trying to be happy! And look what you just did to her!"

"Get out before I shoot you," Pandora darted, as fire blazed through her eyes.

"Shoot me then!" He hollered in her face.

Quinn snatched a couple of towels, grabbed Eden by the arm and hauled her out of the room. She had been down this road with Pandora and Bruce too many times in college and she knew things were about to get ugly.

"And she had the nerve to damn *me* to hell for sleeping with somebody's husband," Eden scurried behind Quinn, closing what was left of the door. Pandora pushed through Bruce and rushed to grab her purse, but he gripped her waist and threw her against the wall.

"Don't touch me!" She screamed, punching him clean in the face with her wedding ring. Bruce grabbed his face as blood shot out from his nose. "After you cheated on me like that in college. *You* did this to us. Not me!" Tears of anger and hurt began to surface from her eyes.

Lifting a nearby chair, she flung it in his direction, hitting him in the chest. Bruce barely even flinched from the hard blow. Wiping the blood from his nose, he darted over to her like he could snatch the life out of her body.

"I hate you so much! Get out," Pandora continued to scream, throwing kicks and punches. Bruce breathed heavily through his demented glare, taking everything she threw. Her emotions filled the room and tears tore from her eyes. She wanted to kill him and kiss him at the same time. They'd gone through so much together, yet

they still couldn't find a way to hate one another. Bruce
was bloody, beat up, and pissed off, but Pandora
was *still* the love of his life. He could see the beauty
through the raging beast he'd brought out of her, and he
was sick of fighting. He gripped her hands to prevent her
from punching him any longer.

"Tell me why you're so angry at me,"

"Get *off* of me!" She growled. Pandora tried to knee him,
but he grabbed her leg and hitched it around his waist.
Reaching down, he kissed her. Shock and confusion
gripped her tongue for a moment. They'd gone from
impersonal enemies, to searingly intimate in a heartbeat.
Regaining her composure, Pandora pushed against him,
but he followed and kissed her again. "Stop it!"

"*You stop*," he demanded. She tried breaking free a
second time, but Bruce locked her against the wall with
his heavy frame. He was in her personal space. Too
intimate, and far too familiar.

"Bruce," she calmed down, trying to control her
emotions.

"How long are you going to pretend like you don't love
me, Anna?" He whispered against her ear. Her eyes slid
closed as Bruce spoke her name in a way that set her off
like only he could. He smelled delicious, the subtle
fragrance of his Gucci Guilty cologne mixed with the
virile scent that was his alone. Pandora temporarily
folded, wallowing in him the way she used to. She
pressed her body into his until even air couldn't come
between them. Holding her still, he began to eat away at
her mouth, sliding his lips back and forth across hers.
Bruce turned a simple kiss into an erotic melding that left

Pandora trembling. Just before she let go completely, a tiny voice of caution screamed through her pleasure. She remembered his ex-wife, the airport, the lies, the pain, and why she walked away from him in the first place.

"We should stop," she breathed heavily, regaining control of her leg as she forced his body to back away from her.

"You don't want to stop," he followed her back against the wall.

"You remember how much I cared about you?" He whispered at her mouth.

"I remember how much you hurt me."

"I remember how much I worshipped you."

Bruce lifted her chin and kissed her soft lips until her body could no longer contain the ferocious swell of emotions that needed to be released; the love, the anger, the fear, and the pain. *God*, the pain.

"Kiss me back," he ordered. "Touch me the way you once had a right to." Staring into his eyes, Pandora kissed him back, nearly tearing into him. Bruce slid his hands down her tiny, bare waist as goosebumps began to dot her skin. She pulled at his head trying to urge him away but she was fighting to get closer at the same time.

"Bruce," she gasped against his mouth. She had a husband, another life, and vows to think about, but her mind had become too cloudy to protest. It was like being on the best roller coaster ride ever. As the climb began, neither of them could believe what the heck they were thinking, but it was too late for backing out now. Bruce made her forget herself. *He made her want to forget everything*. He had her under siege, seducing her with a

171

monumental feeling she hadn't felt in years. *And she surrendered.*

"Take his ring off your finger," his gaze drank her in, "You don't belong to him. You belong to me *and I want you back.*" Pandora reached for her wedding bands almost innately and did what she was told.

Moments later, they both became a writhing, pulsating mass of pleasure. Moans and gasps filled the room as they grinded through clutching limbs and contracting muscles. Pandora opened her balled fist and clawed the bedsheets, sending the wedding rings she held in her hands over the edge.

Chapter 11

Oh, the tangled web we weave...

Over the next two months, Bruce and Pandora spent every waking moment together. After they'd gotten four years of sexual frustration out of their system at the convention, neither of them bothered to do it again. The pleasure they shared came from the *lover*, not the sex. They found satisfaction in just being in each other's presence. They met up for Starbucks in the morning, lunch in the afternoon, and late dinners after work. When Jackson was away, Pandora turned off her security cameras and allowed Bruce to stay in her home. They showered together, stayed up half the night talking, and fell asleep in each other's arms with the intention to wake up and do it all over the next day.

While Pandora loved her husband to the moon and back, no man in her life had ever come close to Bruce. There was a time in her marriage when Jackson would travel for work, and she'd be disappointed not being able to see him for a week. Now, she looked forward to it because it meant she didn't have to lie to his face and sneak around behind his back. During their time together, Bruce sent Savanna packing. Minus her tantrum at the convention, she and Bruce had a fairly good relationship.

But he refused to break another woman's heart trying to fill a void that could only be filled by one person; *Pandora*.

Bruce also caught Pandora up on the last four years of his life and how his ex-wife had made his finances a living hell. After divorcing her, Angela found a way to get a large alimony check from Bruce each month in addition to ridiculous child support payments. Angela had a new boyfriend, and together they were living off of Bruce's income. Bruce made excellent money as a detective, but Angela was killing his pockets and Pandora didn't like it. She put important clients and major business deals on hold to dig into his case and find out what was really going on. After thorough research, Pandora discovered that Angela's new boyfriend was actually her husband, and had been so for the last two years. They'd gotten married out of the country and never processed their paperwork in the United States because their legal marriage would mean the end of Bruce's support.

Pandora worked her magic, got hold of Angela's marriage certificate and sent it to a judge in California who'd been handling their case. Almost immediately, Bruce was set free from Angela's fraud and deception. The judge also forced her and her new husband to pay Bruce back for the two years she'd been married, which totaled up to over three hundred thousand dollars. For her time, generosity, and loss of money she suffered from missing clients, Bruce gave Pandora half of it even though she begged him not too. Bruce also dug deeper into Eden's case, and still, there were missing pieces of information that had yet to be discovered. His next move was to investigate Jackson, but he knew Pandora would have a fit, so, he promised to leave him out of it. Together, Bruce and Pandora were a powerful team and living proof that while true love may lie dormant for a while, it *never* dies. It survived and lived on no matter what.

Pandora sat in Bruce's lap in the office of her bedroom working on her computer as he ran his fingers through her hair and planted kisses on her neck.

"Can I tell you something?" He stroked her cheek.

"What's up?"

"I want to spend the rest of my life with you."

Pandora slowed down her typing and cut her eyes at Bruce.

"Listen, before you freak out, I know firsthand that leaving a marriage and another life is a hard pill to swallow. I've also learned that being honest with your heart feels so much better than living a lie."

"I'm not freaking out," Pandora turned to face him. "I've been thinking about *us* a lot. I've also been thinking about Jackson. I don't—" she hesitated, "I feel stuck. I understand the battle your heart dealt with in your own marriage now, and I regret putting you through it. Now, the shoe is on the other foot and I don't know what to do."

"Why though? What happened to us? Why didn't we fix it when we had the chance?" Bruce asked.

"You need to ask yourself that. I came back to you in college like you asked and you cheated on me, Bruce."

"Why do you keep saying *I* cheated on *you*?"

Bruce sat up, confused. *"I didn't."*

"Are you serious?" Pandora pursed her lips. "After all these years, you still refuse to tell the truth?"

"Joanna, I saw you with my own eyes. I came up to your room after football practice and you were screwing one of my teammates. After I waited *two years* for you—*Two-* And you stabbed me in the back like I meant nothing."

Pandora jerked her head back and winced.

"Don't give me that look. Yes, I saw you that night, so I got even the next day."

"What do you mean you caught *me* sleeping with someone else? I was sleeping with you!"

Bruce flung his arms into the air and laughed. "Come on, man. You're a defense attorney. You can't find a better lie than that?"

"I promise I'm not lying," Pandora gave him an incredulous stare. "I sent you a text b*egging* you to come to my room that night. I had a few drinks and I was ready to let loose. I told you to wear your football helmet and those tight uniform pants I loved seeing you play in. You never replied, but you came into my room." She shook her head trying to ward off the shock. "Or at least I *thought* it was you…*it felt like you.*"

Their eyes studied one another as if they were searching for the truth. Bruce's lips pressed together in a slight grimace as he thought back to that night.

"Baby, I never got any messages from you. We had an away game and I left my phone in Andr—" Bruce's eyes and mouth shot open.

"What?"

I know damn well he didn't..." Bruce sat straight up trying to wrap his mind around his thoughts. "Anna, promise me you're not blowing smoke up my behind."

"I promise," She furrowed, annoyed, "What would it benefit me to lie about something that happened over a decade ago?"

Bruce crouched forward and balled his fists. Veins protruded in his head and throbbed in his throat. He looked like an angry bull ready to attack.

Pandora looked at him. "What in the world ha—"

The front door slamming caused both of them to jump.

"Joanna!" Jackson's thunderous voice rang out from downstairs.

Pandora jumped up from Bruce's lap looking like she'd just heard the devil call her name.

"I thought you said he wouldn't be back until later," Bruce leaped up from the chair, quickly scanning the area for someplace to hide.

"He wasn't. I was supposed to pick him up from the airport at 3. It's—" she looked down at her watch and realized it was after 6:30. Her eyes bulged. "Shoot!"

Jackson stomped up the stairs.

"Get under my desk. He doesn't come in here." Bruce disappeared under her desk and Pandora rushed out of her office door just as Jackson entered into the room looking like a mad man.

"Are you *serious* right now?" He snapped.

"Baby, I'm sorry," she grabbed her head with her hands. "I was doing work and completely lost track of time."

"I called you *fifty* times. I called your office. I called the house. I called Quinn. *Nobody* knew where you were."

"I was home in the office," she pointed. "I didn't hear the phone ring, and my cell is," she fished around her pocket for her cellphone. "Shoot, I don't know. It's probably still in my car."

"What's up with you?" Frustrated, Jackson threw his bag across the room. It hit the dresser and knocked down every perfume bottle Pandora owned.

"Really?" Pandora shook her head.

"Yes, really! I have a right to be upset and destroy stuff. You've been acting like this for almost two *months* now."

"Acting like what?"

"You leave early. You come home late. You tell me you're one place, but I call and find out you're not there. I don't hear from you when I go away, you barely even *look* at me anymore, and I can't even remember the last time we had sex. You don't touch me. You're not happy to see me. *Nothing*. Now, you can't even remember to pick me up from the airport!"

"Jackson, I'm sorry," she defended, feeling guilty.

"Where are your wedding rings?" He pointed angrily at her ring finger. "I haven't seen them since you came back from your retreat."

"What do you mean, it's right—" her eyes dropped down to her ring finger and she realized it was bare. Suddenly, it hit her. Bruce had sexed her out of them and she was so gone out of her mind, she never did pick them up from the floor. In that moment Pandora felt like the world's biggest whore. Rubbing the back of her neck, her eyes peered up at Jackson and her world came crashing into a guilty focus. She felt selfish, sneaky, and just plain wrong. She nearly wrecked her friendship with Eden to be with Jackson, and her loyalty to him didn't even last 24 months.

"Anna, talk to me. Seriously, what's going on with you?" Jackson walked into her and lifted her chin to face him, but she stepped back and looked in another direction. She couldn't face him. "Am I making you unhappy? Are you upset with me about something?"

"No, I just. My mind is all over the place. I'll do better. I promise."

Jackson put his hands around her hips.

Pandora tried to back up but Jackson pushed her toward the bed.

"Kiss me," he ordered. "Look at me like you used to. Kiss me like you used to." Pandora looked up at him and wanted to cry. She never felt so guilty in her entire life. She didn't want to kiss him, touch him, or do anything else. She wanted to run away. However, to keep the peace and distract him long enough for Bruce to find an exit, she did what she was asked. Jackson bent down and kissed her softly.

"I miss you," she lied.

"Show me how much." Jackson lifted her skirt above her waist, exposing her black thong. He laid her down on the bed as he placed kisses all over her body. His erection was loaded and ready for takeoff. Pulling himself out of his shorts, he slid her thong to the side and tried to make his way into her. He didn't get very far, however, because for the first time ever, she wasn't moist enough to allow him in. *Her body didn't want him anymore.* This upset him. When he finally did get it in, Pandora felt different.

For the last five years, Pandora's insides had curved to him, but now it appeared someone else had left their imprint. Jackson was no fool. Angry, his pride and ego got the best of him. His normally calm and pleasant demeanor began to shift, and his face contorted into an all-consuming rage. His nostrils flared, and his vengeful eyes closed into slits. His mouth quivered, slurring words that were incoherent. He risked *everything* to be with Pandora, and she was being unfaithful? Before Jackson knew it, his anger had erupted like a volcano and he was bulldozing through her kitten like he was a mad man. He could hear Pandora steadily begging for him to either stop or slow down, but that just made him go harder and faster. Suddenly, something inside of him snapped and he grabbed a hold of her throat and pressed down on her neck.

"Whoever he is, you'd better end it*!"* He threatened, crashing into her. The sound of a gun going off bought him back to reality. When he finally looked down, Pandora was choking and her face was full of tears. Her eyes were laced with a type of fear he'd never seen on a human being. This scared

him. *Did I almost kill her*? He thought. The weight of his heavy body had rushed the flow of air right out of Pandora's chest, but that didn't stop her from pushing him back to catch her breath.

"Get the hell off of me!" She screamed, crawling

back to safety.

Jackson fixed his pants, staring at Pandora with sheer panic. He couldn't believe he zoned out like that.

"Baby, wait. I blacked out. I don't know what happened." He reached for her but she used her left heel to kick him in his crotch as hard as she possibly could. The force sent Jackson flying off the bed at what seemed like the speed of light. He fell to the floor like a sack of potatoes and his head made contact with the nightstand beside their bed.

"Get out! *Now!*" Pandora pointed sharply at the door.

Jackson didn't even bother to argue with her anymore because he knew he was dead wrong. Getting up from the floor, he blinked his eyes rapidly trying to ward off the shock of his actions. He turned to look at Pandora but he could see she was shaken up and terrified. Tears welled up in his eyes, but he left the room, rushed down the steps and out the front door.

The second Pandora heard the front door slam, all of her strength left her and she fell into the floor crying. Bruce came rushing out of her office like a swarm of hornets with his gun in his hand. He didn't know if Jackson had left or not, but for Jackson's sake, he hoped he did. Bruce fired a warning shot out of the open window by the desk, but it took everything in his power not to send it right into Jackson's skull.

"Are you alright?" He asked, shaken up.

Pandora's mind raced down memory lane, back into the Perkins' dungeon. Suddenly, she began to hyperventilate and overheat. Her face turned red as she gasped for air.

"Anna," Bruce got down to the ground, urgently snatching her into his grasp. "Baby, you're having a panic attack. I need you to try and relax."

Pandora couldn't relax if her life depended on it. She couldn't stand, she couldn't breathe and she couldn't speak. All she felt was an intense, debilitating pain surfacing through her body. She felt like she was trying to run from the scariest thing in her life, but couldn't. Her vision was spotty and with each gasp for air, she felt like she was suffocating.

"Joanna!" Bruce said sternly. "Take slower breaths or you're gonna end up passing out from a lack of oxygen." He gripped her into a firm hug and coached her to breathe normally. He could feel her heart thrashing in her chest and it made him writhe. He wanted to rip Jackson limb from limb. After a few minutes of coaching, Pandora started to breathe easier, but her tears overshadowed it. Securing her arms tightly around Bruce's neck, she cried a gut-wrenching cry that almost choked the life out of Bruce. He hugged her back and tried to remain calm, but he couldn't. Focusing on a nearby wall, his eyes looked like weapons. He was *livid*. Bruce knew there was something in Eden's case that just wasn't making any sense. All signs pointed to Jackson, but he had remained faithful to his promise to keep him out of it. But after today, all bets and promises were off.

Two hours later…

Pandora decided to stay the rest of the week with

Quinn. After putting her pajamas on and tossing her overnight bag in Quinn's guest bedroom closet, she walked into Quinn's bedroom and got into the bed beside her.

"I feel so bad putting Andre out of his room."

"You've put him out of the clubhouse in elementary school, made him move his seat during lunch in high school, and threw him out of his own dorm in college...how nice of you to feel terrible about it twenty-five years later," Quinn giggled.

"Those were crucial moments and I needed you."

"He's fine. He understands."

"I'm seriously caught in a web and can't find my way out. Quinn, I've *never* been a woman that cheats or really understood why people do it. I gave my all to Jackson. I don't know what changed all of a sudden."

"Oh the tangled web we weave, when we first practice to deceive," Quinn shook her head. "You've *never* given your all to Jackson. *Ever*. Your relationship was built on lies, deception, and cheating. You barely saw one another, and to this day you're comfortable being away from him. *All the time*. He knows nothing about your past, nothing about your family."

"It wasn't intentional," Pandora defended. "It wasn't like I was purposely trying to hide my past. I just let it go. It's not who I am anymore and it holds no kind of importance in my space."

"Your past *is* a part of who you are," Quinn held her hand. "It may not affect you in a negative way, but it's what helped mold and shape you into who you are. It's okay to acknowledge that. But you're married. When you get married, you exchange your *I*'s for a *we* and become one. You and Jackson were never one with each other, and you never will be as long as your heart is lost in somebody else's world."

"I know you're probably upset that I waited this long to finally tell you about Bruce," Pandora lowered her head in guilt. "I've wanted to tell you for the longest time. I've tried, but I could never get the words out."

"Actually, y*ou* didn't tell us- *he* did," Quinn raised an eyebrow and crossed her arms.

"You're not gonna make this easy, are you?"

"No," Quinn gawked. "I love you, but you've stepped in it big time. And the fact that you couldn't tell us proves that you *still*, to this day, strive to create a false picture of perfection and you need to stop. Get *real*. No one is perfect. We all make mistakes. Let she who is without sin stop *lying* to herself. The mere fact that you have two very flawed friends and you didn't feel comfortable enough to show your o*wn* true face is sad."

Pandora sighed. "I know."

"*Especially* considering the way you handled Eden after her mix-up with Joseph. You ripped that girl a new behind, and now you're intruding on my lovemaking time looking for grace and a way out."

"Listen, I feel terrible. I had one man hiding under my computer, and another one so angry and confused he basically violated me. Everything is wrong and I need to make it right before this spirals out of control."

"Honey, control is a fading memory. The situation was out of control when you slept with a married man for eight years. Control ran for the hills when you used

Jackson as a jump-off to get over Bruce, and it disappeared altogether when you married him and then cheated on him with the same guy you were running from this whole time." Quinn shook her head in disbelief. "What a *mess*."

"I always thought of myself as a good person. I feel like the scum of the earth now." Tears welled in Pandora's eyes as she lowered her head and melted into the bed.

"You *are* a good person," Quinn laid down with her. "Good people put themselves in bad situations. I've done it. But in order to fix it, you've got to hold yourself accountable. Isn't that what we taught Eden? People will drive you crazy if you allow them, but 99.9 percent of the time we hand over the keys."

"I bashed Jackson for being a liar and a cheat, and now I'm a liar and a cheater just like him," Pandora wiped her hands down her frustrated face. "I've brought all of this on myself. I just want to wake up and *everything* be back to normal."

"But what is your version of normal? Do you want your husband or do you want Bruce? Jackson loves you. Considering everything he's done in the past, I'm sure he'd be willing to forgive and move forward at some point. But is it him you *really* want to move forward with?"

Pandora stared into space. She already knew the answer. Quinn did too.

"I didn't think so," Quinn said sweetly.

Without warning, the realization of everything Pandora had done to try and hide from Bruce came crashing into her. Quinn held her and consoled her while she faced it all and cried for nearly thirty minutes. Her heart was *always* with Bruce. Nothing had changed. Nothing would *ever* change.

"Am I wrong?" She finally asked.

"Absolutely not," Quinn responded immediately. "You and Bruce are amazing together. You've always been perfect for one another. For years, you two found a way to love and kept on loving through everything life handed you. That's what marriage is, *endurance*. Unfortunately, you both are stubborn and somehow keep denying yourselves what you really want, which is each other. You've allowed your egos, selfishness, and pride to drag children and other people's hearts into your foolishness, and it's now a big mess. If you two want each other, you need to stop the charade and *be* together."

"But is it that easy to just divorce my husband?"

"It was that easy for you to marry him. We've all reacted stupidly at one point or another, but trifling is trifling. You get what you give, and right now you're giving love a black eye."

"At the time, Jackson was what I thought I needed, Quinn. Coming into grips with the realization that Bruce was married with children was hard. It didn't stop me from loving him, but being the other woman ate me alive. I got caught up in him and couldn't find a way out. When I was finally bold enough to do it, I needed a distraction that would keep me away for good."

"My sentiments, exactly." Quinn nodded. "You had a wounded heart, which, oftentimes makes us behave uncharacteristically. You never healed or grieved from

Bruce. You need to do some serious personal development work or you'll end up recreating different versions of this situation with another man. If you find a way out of this and Bruce is who you want, *have him*. Get married; stop it with the breaking up and getting back together. It's ridiculous and draining. You also owe Jackson the truth. No one deserves deception. If—"

Grabbing her stomach, Pandora got up and rushed into Quinn's master bathroom. She barely made it to the toilet before she knelt over and puked her guts out.

"Ew," Quinn winced.

"Sorry. I don't know what's wrong with me. I've been queasy and throwing up all week," Pandora flushed the toilet and turned on the sink to splash water on her face. "Anyway, what were you saying?" She sat down in the bathroom and leaned against the wall trying to get herself together.

"I was saying you need to tell Jackson what's going on. Being honest like that will feel like death, but you won't break."

"I love Bruce, but what if we just aren't meant to be, you know? What if fixing things with Jackson and finding a way over Bruce is the better option?"

"Those are questions you have to answer for yourself. The good news is that—" Quinn's speech was interrupted a second time by the sounds of Pandora projectile vomiting in her toilet. Furrowing her eyebrows, she got up and walked inside. "Are you alright?"

"I don't know. Maybe it's my nerves."

"Have you been to the doctors lately?"

"No. I'm not in any debilitating pain. I'm telling

you it's my nerves. This used to happen to me in law school all the time."

"You've been over the top emotional lately," Quinn looked at her. " I don't think I've ever seen you cry so much in my life. And now you're sick."

Pandora turned her head toward the toilet and heaved some more.

"I'll be right back." Quinn walked away and returned five minutes later with a glass of Pedialyte and a pregnancy test.

"Mannequin, don't play with me. Yeah, right." Pandora sat by the toilet seat darting her eyes at Quinn.

"Drink it, and take it," Quinn ordered, handing everything over to her.

"I'm not pregnant. I'm not taking this stupid test; it would be a slap in the face."

"Your symptoms are telling me differently."

Pandora drank the Pedialyte and took the test out of her hand. "I haven't taken one of these things since high school. I feel so silly."

"I'm gonna go check on Andre. Call me when you're done." Quinn got up and walked out of the bathroom.

Of all the things that could be wrong, she suggests pregnancy. Pandora stared down at the test. *There's no way*. Getting up from the floor, she opened the test and followed the instructions.

Quinn walked through her corridor and into her

husband's office. "Hey you."

"Hey," Andre glanced up with a smile.

"You all finished with your sermon?" She walked over and sat on his lap.

"Just about, why? Are you ready for me?"

"I'm always ready for you," she flirted, planting soft kisses on his neck.

Andre dropped his pen and blushed. Quinn had an entirely different side to her behind closed doors. It was such a turn on that he was the only person to ever see it. Just as he went to kiss her back, a loud, horrific blood-curling scream that couldn't have possibly been human sounded from their bedroom. Quinn and Andre's eyes snapped open. Quinn jumped up with excitement.

"I'll be right back," she raced down the hall and back into her bedroom.

Pandora stood in the doorway staring at the positive pregnancy test with glazed eyes.

Quinn grabbed the stick and leaped for joy. "I knew it. Congratulations!" She fanned herself as tears rushed down her face.

Pandora didn't know what to think or how to react. She dragged herself toward the bed, knocking things off of Quinn's dresser trying to grab something to hold onto. *Pregnant? Me?* She thought back to the last time she and Jackson slept together and realized there was no way this baby could belong to him. She sat down on the bed as Quinn sat next to her. They both stared at the test in awe. Suddenly, she felt like the last fifteen years of her life had been erased and she was standing back in the Penny Pack

Park anticipating the future with the boy of her dreams. Indeed, she was pregnant...*with Bruce's baby.*

Chapter 12

"You can run with a lie, but you can't hide from the truth. It will catch you!"

After going through four boxes of positive pregnancy tests, Pandora still couldn't come to grips with her new reality. She spent the rest of the week going to doctor's appointments, taking Quinn along for support. The brutal, continuous rape she suffered at the hands of the Perkins' destroyed her ovaries and fallopian tubes. *"Even if I perform every technology we have, you'll never be able to have kids,"* she remembered her doctor saying. Those words haunted her for years. It was horrible enough being held prisoner in someone's dungeon, but the idea that she was also infertile was devastating to bear.

Since the day Pandora had fallen in love with Bruce, she had dreams of getting married, having children, and growing old together. Throughout their childhood, they'd argue over where they would live, where they'd go to school, and what their unborn children's names would be. When she became pregnant the first time, she was afraid but excited. Life hadn't happened in the time frame she wanted it too, but it was happening and that was all that mattered.

The day she saw Bruce at the convention was the hardest moment of her life. Another woman had taken her place and was living her life. She blamed herself at first. If fate had only given them their baby, they'd still be together. She felt like half a woman after that. She felt like she was broken and couldn't be fixed, like her body had betrayed her. Now, after blood work and multiple hormone tests, what she had been told was impossible since she was sixteen-years-old, had come into fruition. This wasn't a fluke. This wasn't a dream, and she wasn't being punked. She was going to be a mother.

Pandora had ignored Jackson and Bruce's phone calls all week, and now it was time to go back home to face the music. Before letting anyone know about her pregnancy, she wanted to make things right. Pandora called Bruce and expressed how much she loved him, but that her marriage came first. She requested that all communication be cut between them for a while so she could tell her husband everything she'd been doing. If after that, her heart still led her to him, then she would follow it.

"Just as your spirit to fight and go on has preserved you in the past, your faith and trust in God will get you through the test of the future," Quinn said as Pandora unlocked her front door and walked into her home.

"We'll see. I just got home, so I'll call you later. Thanks for everything." She blew kisses into the phone before hanging up.

Dropping her purse and car keys on the table, she walked into her living room to see Jackson sitting on the couch waiting for her. As soon as he saw her, he quickly stood up.

"Hey," she spoke softly.

"Hey," he walked over, planting a hesitant kiss on her cheek. "I got your text."

"Good. How are you?" Pandora sat down on the couch as Jackson nervously followed suit.

"Not well at all. I feel like crap for what happened last week and you have every right to hate me."

"I don't hate you. I *will* kill you if you ever violate me like that again, but I don't hate you."

Jackson raised an eyebrow at Pandora's straight face and saw she was serious.

"What's happening to us?" Jackson asked. "I miss you; all the arguing and fighting. This house feels so cold. One day we were fine, and the next it was like you wouldn't even look at me the same."

"I slept with someone else," her voice shook, finally getting it out. The entire room grew deadly silent.

With a slacked mouth, Jackson openly stared at Pandora. He was speechless. The sadness and shock in his eyes nearly deflated her. He knew deep down she had stepped out on him, but to hear her confess it was earth-shattering.

"Wow..." was the only word his defeated heart could express.

"There was someone in my life long before I knew you existed. He was the only man I'd ever given my heart too. We dated on and off from middle school to college," she wiped away a forming tear, "and he ended up getting married on me. I couldn't let him go, and we ended up sneaking around the entire eight years he was married. Eventually, he left his wife for me but at that point, I just

wanted to experience life without him. And I found you."
Jackson was floored.

"So, what was I? Some kind of rebound? Flunky?"

"You were an escape," she replied honestly, "and you were good for me. I loved you. I cared about you. I fought for what I thought my heart wanted. I almost lost a friend, my dignity, *everything*. I put it all on the line for *you*, and to prove to the whole world that I could live happily ever after...without *him*." More tears flowed from her eyes as she peered into Jackson's. "But I couldn't do it. He popped up again, and I folded. I'm sorry for doing this to us."

Jackson took in an angry, deep breath. It didn't matter that he'd cheated on Pandora with Eden their entire relationship, or that he murdered his own daughter. It didn't matter that he'd been sleeping with Jade and paying her to hack into Pandora's computer on a daily basis. What mattered was that he was sadistically in love with Pandora, and it would be a chilly day in hell before another man took what belonged to him.

"Who is he?" Jackson licked his lips, trying to swallow his anger.

"You don't know him. You've never met him."

"Does he work with you? What is he, some hotshot lawyer too?" His voice was laced with jealousy.

"No, and no," Pandora replied with a swift head nod. "That's not really important at this point. He didn't do anything other than be bold enough to ask for what he wanted. I'm the one who consented. I'm the one that's married. I'm the one at fault."

Jackson made a mental note to hire a private

investigator to find out who *he* was. *He* was going to die a slow death.

"So where do we go from here?"

"I...I don't know."

"You're my wife, Anna. I'm angry, I'm hurt, but I married you for better or for worse. It's gonna take some time, but we'll find a way to move forward."

"Before you settle on that decision, there's something else I have to tell you."

"What?"

"Last week I found out," she lowered her head. "I...I found out I was—" a knock sounded at the front door, interrupting her confession.

"Who is that?" He leaned to look out the window but didn't see anyone. "Are you expecting someone?"

"No," Pandora shook her head.

"Oh wait, you know what? Mike said he'd drop by some paperwork," Jackson stood up. "That's probably him."

"I'm gonna go grab a drink and use the restroom. I'll be back." She got up and walked down the hall into the kitchen.

Jackson walked over to the front door and answered it. He looked a bit startled when he realized it wasn't his co-worker Mike.

"Hello?"

"Hey, neighbor," a man dressed in sweatpants and a black t-shirt stood at the door.

"Neighbor?"

"Well, sort of. I'm Josh. I live about a mile up the road. My tire just popped," he moved to the side so

Jackson could see his car. "And of course when I need my cell, it's dead. I was wondering if I could use your phone to call Triple-A."

Jackson looked at the man's car and then looked at him. He seemed sincere, but Jackson didn't trust giving out his cell. He'd done it once before and a thief ran off with it. "We have a house phone you can use." He stepped aside to let Josh in. "I'm Jackson, by the way."

Josh stepped up the rest of the stairs and made his way into the house, extending his hand for Jackson to shake it. "Thanks, man, I appreciate it." He followed Jackson into the kitchen.

"There's the phone right on the wall."

"How's Mike doing?" Pandora hollered down the hall.

"It wasn't Mike, baby. It's a neighbor. He wanted to use our phone."

"Neighbor? Why would the neighbor need to—" she entered into the kitchen and nearly fainted when she saw Bruce standing there with her home phone in his hand.

"This is Josh. He's from up the road. His tire popped. Josh, this is my wife, Anna."

"Nice to meet you," Bruce nodded, pulling out his wallet.

"While you're waiting, I have some tools and a spare tire for your busted wheel. We may finish before Triple-A gets here," Jackson said.

"That's even better," Bruce looked up, grateful. "Thanks, man."

Jackson left the kitchen and made his way to the

garage. Pandora looked at Bruce like he had lost his mind.

"What *mess* are you trying to start?" She gritted through her teeth.

Bruce pulled a mini walkie talkie from his back pocket.

"Officers, door is open. Come in." He looked at Pandora. "I need you to back up and keep your mouth shut," Bruce warned just as Jackson came back into the kitchen.

"I just realized I lent my tools out. Sorry about that."

"It's quite alright. I'm not really here to use your phone, and I'm not your neighbor from up the road." Two police officers walked into the house and made their way into the kitchen. Jackson furrowed.

"I'm Detective Steed," he pulled out his badge, "and you sir, are under arrest."

"Excuse me?" Jackson jerked his head back. "For what?"

"For the murder of an unborn fetus, the attempted murder of Eden Grant, and conspiracy to commit the murder of Ruby Grant."

Pandora's eyes widened.

"What the hell?" Jackson fussed, "Are you serious?"

"Well, I'm no lawyer, but I believe fetal homicide, two counts of murder, and first-degree murder are pretty serious," he responded coldly. The police rushed over and pinned him to the wall. "You have the right to remain silent. Anything you say- can and will be used against you in a court of law."

"Anna! Tell them to—" the police officers handcuffed him and proceeded to push him toward the front door.

"You have the right to an attorney. If you cannot afford an attorney, one will be appointed for you."

Pandora stood back, watching in horrific confusion.

Bruce pulled out a thick Manila envelope from the back of his sweatshirt and dropped it on the kitchen counter. "Everything you need to know is in here." Bruce followed the officers out of the house trying to detain Jackson as he cursed and fought them off.

Dumbfounded, Pandora's eyes dropped down to the envelope.

Chapter 13

Pandora's Box

Over the next month and a half, it seemed as if Pandora had dropped off the face of the earth. Her employees came to work as scheduled, *but she didn't.* Important clients were forced to seek help from other law firms due to canceled meetings and no-show appointments. Pandora's assistants cringed every day as they were met with dial tones and profanity from angry clients who had been on her waiting list for months that had to be passed down to other lawyers in her firm. Hundreds of thousands of dollars walked into her place of business looking for help, but turned around and walked out the minute they realized the head honcho was unavailable.

Pandora even backed out of a high profile case that she'd been working on for almost a year. PJ, one of the most dangerous Jamaican drug lords in Virginia had been convicted of drug trafficking, assault and battery, murder, money laundering, fraud, embezzlement, theft, pandering, and other serious charges that would've put him away for a long time. Pandora had all her chips lined up to have his record cleared and his charges dropped. Two days before the trial began, Pandora disappeared. PJ was forced to use a public defender that lost the case, making him guilty and sentenced to over twenty-five years in prison. Word traveled quickly about the many death threats being sent into Pandora's office from PJ's men. Many people believed PJ was the reason for her sudden disappearance, but no one knew for sure.

Bruce hadn't been able to contact her either. After everything he'd shown her in that envelope, Bruce knew it would take her some time to digest, but after six weeks of ignoring his phone calls, emails, text messages, and voicemails, he was beginning to worry. He'd gone to her home, but even that looked deserted. He tried tracking her car but found it in her garage. As a last resort, he went to Quinn. After swearing her to secrecy from Eden and confidentiality from the rest of the world, Bruce let Quinn know everything he'd discovered. For a psychologist who had just about heard it all, this left her *floored*.

"Wha-*what*? Are you— *wait*. How can—" were the only words her raspy, barely audible, voice could speak before her mind began to buzz. Immediately, she grew nauseous and lightheaded. Bruce had to escort her to the nearest chair before she passed out. Her body was so stiff that he had to keep checking to make sure she was still breathing. After that, her mind didn't know how to react, so it just sort of shut down.

Quinn's face went slack, her mouth slightly opened and all the color drained from her face as she stared wide-eyed into space. It took her almost a week to wrap her mind around the truth. She was scared for Eden and blamed herself for putting her in the line of fire a second time by bringing Jade into her home. Quinn remembered the way Eden looked at Jackson the day she came home from the hospital and the fear in her eyes when she saw Jade in her home. *Did Eden know the truth? If so, how come she hadn't said anything yet? Had she tried and I missed it?* Quinn did everything she could to help find Pandora, but even *she* had no luck.

She checked Pandora's house in Virginia, the one in Maryland, and the beach house she owned by the shore. *Nothing.* She even checked the local psych wards, assuming Pandora had lost her mind. No luck there either.

Bruce saw to it that Jackson was housed in a low profile facility. He wanted to make sure he'd captured all the pieces to Jackson's sick puzzle before the media and press got involved and complicated things. He also wanted to protect Pandora for as long as he possibly could.

Bruce was an amazing detective and did his job well, but this bust was bittersweet. Cracking a huge case resulting in the capture of a criminal meant a good run for his career, but it also meant sabotage for the woman he loved; the mother of his child that he still had no knowledge of. Once things escalated to a national level, Pandora's career and dignity would be crushed. It would provoke the feds to investigate her to find out if she was a part of the crimes, and the media would have a *field* day with it. Who would trust a lawyer that married a murderer, resulting in the escape of a prisoner and the death of an innocent woman and her granddaughter?

The paparazzi often captured photos of Eden,

Pandora, and Quinn together, so the world knew of their friendship. It wouldn't take long for the tabloids to piece together Pandora's deception and disloyalty to Eden by marrying her child's father. Things were about to get *very* ugly, *very* quickly and Bruce only hoped Pandora would still love him after the dust settled.

Jade sat in the waiting room of the Virginia School of Medicine awaiting her interview. After a few failed attempts at Netflix and chill, Dwayne finally softened up after Pandora went missing and gave Jade what she wanted. The good sex they had was right on time because Jade hadn't been able to get in touch with Jackson for almost two months and she was beginning to get sexually frustrated. She wanted to quit her assistantship with Pandora, but she needed the money. Instead, she held on to the job but looked to Dwayne to prep her for her interview. After their month-long rendezvous, Jade started to really like Dwayne and hoped they could be more than just sex buddies and good company.

Dwayne however, wasn't interested. With no kids, no wife, and nothing standing in his way, he decided to quit his job on the medical school board and take a higher paying position in Africa writing grant proposals and finding scholarship funding for low-income communities. Jade was sad, but she understood. She missed Travis a lot, and Dwayne was the only guy she'd met since she'd come to Virginia that was worth any of her time. As a final promise, Dwayne ensured that he'd be there for her interview to see to it that Jade got accepted, and he held true to his word. Jade crossed her leg and smiled from ear to ear the second she spotted Dwayne walking into the conference room. He took his seat amongst the rest of the board judges.

"*That's* Dwayne?" Lauren, Jade's friend she'd met at a local bar, asked.

"That's him…" Jade smiled.

"He is sexy," Lauren gazed intensely through the window. "Does he have any friends?"

"No," Jade winced, frowning at Lauren. "The last thing you need is to be introduced to any more men after that stunt you pulled at the strip club. That's why we're going to get you tested now."

"Relax. I was just trying to lighten my mood."

"I just— *I'm sorry*," Jade shook her head. "I can't believe you actually slept with that stripper *unprotected.* Lauren, you could have contracted anything from him."

"I told you, I knew Derrick before he became a stripper. Not that it makes everything okay, but I was drunk and horny. I didn't have any protection with me."

Being reminded of the story only annoyed Jade further. Rolling her eyes, she grabbed her phone and pulled up her GPS. "Your appointment is about ten minutes away from here, so depending on how long it takes me to ace this interview, we may have to rush."

"Thank you so much for going with me," Lauren lowered her head, embarrassed.

"Girl, I wish you'd told me sooner. Listen, you're twenty-three years old, *I get that*. I was there four years ago. You want to have fun? Have it. Just be smart about it."

"I'm just gonna take a back seat on drinking for now."

"Good. We'll both do it. I tell you what; I'll get tested with you so you don't feel like you're being put on the spot."

"I'd like that," Lauren smiled. "Thanks so much for being there for me without judgment."

"Well, I wouldn't say I didn't judge you…"

They both snickered.

"By the way," Lauren turned to look at Jade, concerned. "Did anyone ever find that lawyer you were working for?"

"Nope," Jade huffed. "Carmen Sandiego is still on the loose."

"That's a shame. What if something happened to her? I heard that drug lord might've her killed and had her body parts sent to different parts of the country."

"Christmas in July," Jade's eyes lit up, hopeful. "Don't tease me like that."

"Well, I want to know what's going on. You know her husband is in jail too?"

Jade snapped her head toward Lauren. "Excuse me?"

"One of my friends used to be a janitor in her office. She talked all the time about your boss's fine husband. Well, she got caught up in some kind of petty theft and got sent to Drinkers for three weeks. Drinkers is like a low budget prison where they keep all the first-time offenders with misdemeanors. She called me the other day and told me *he* was there too."

Jade furrowed her eyebrows, staring at Lauren

with a puzzled glare on her face. She'd been trying to reach Jackson on his other cell phone for a while now and wondered why he hadn't been answering. She assumed he and Pandora had run off on some glorious vacation, which was why they both were missing. But prison?

Something was wrong. Just as Jade's mind began to wander, an assistant from the medical school board came walking out of the conference room.

"Harris?" She called, looking down at her clipboard.

Jade's eyes grew big as she nervously stood up. "I'm Harris."

"Oh good," the woman looked up with a smile. "The board will see you now."

Jade turned to gather her purse and paperwork.

"Good luck Jade, you'll do wonderfully."

"Thanks for the support. I hope so," Jade winked. She followed the woman into the conference room. The room smelled of new carpet and fresh paint. Its cream walls were set off by the brightly colored wallpaper trim, and the billowing wall to ceiling French doors that closed behind her.

"Good Morning, Miss Harris," a board member said.

"Good Morning everyone," Jade gleamed, trying to mask her sudden anxiety.

"Take a seat," Dwayne smiled, flashing Jade a secretive wink.

Jade sat down in the chair as the staff members began to review her application.

"So tell me why you're interested in Medical

School," a woman asked.

"Absolutely. Since I was little, I've had dreams of—" without warning, it seemed as if the bright sun shining into the conference room suddenly disappeared. The room grew a little bit darker and the sky began to roll. The clouds became thick and gray and the wind started to howl, causing some of the board members to glance out the window.

"Is there rain in the forecast?" A board member asked.

"How's that to shake away the anxiety of a med school interview?" another member laughed. "Continue, Miss Harris."

Jade twisted the watch on her wrist and moistened her lips, trying to ward off her nervousness. Just as she went to open her mouth, an eerie quietness overtook the atmosphere. It was ironic and inauspicious- like the calm before a storm.

Time seemed to slow down, and heels could be heard rippling down the hallway with deadly, fluid grace. Jade looked toward the door and locked eyes with what looked like the nucleus of evil.

Pandora strutted to the door like a phantom, terrifying but majestic. Swinging open the French doors, she melted into the doorway like molten gold into a cast.

"*Good afternoon,*" she smirked, her glittering feline eyes trailed around the room.

"Hello," a board member raised an eyebrow in confusion.

Dressed in a combustible mix of five-inch ember-red stilettos, and a figure-hugging, gunpowder black knee-length dress, Pandora pranced into the room in a savage grandeur. "I'm so sorry to interrupt. I hope this isn't anything of *importance,* but Jade, you're fired. I want everything out of my building within the next twenty minutes or I'll have it tossed into the incinerator and burned to *ashes*."

Jade stood straight up, partly afraid and confused. The rest of the board members looked at her strangely, but they knew exactly who Pandora was and valued their jobs enough not to open their mouths.

"Fired? Why?"

"Anna, what are you doing here? This is a private—" Dwayne tried speaking up for Jade, but ate his words when Pandora rutted her eyebrows, daring him to try and make her leave.

"What are you *doing*?" Jade began to cry and her mascara started to run. She was embarrassed, to say the least. "How dare you come here and try to sabotage my career before it even begins?" She screamed to the top of her lungs, lurching toward Pandora as if she wanted to lunge at her.

Pandora didn't flinch. Instead, she found the nearest seat, sat down and crossed her legs, patiently waiting for Jade to try and make a move so she could bash her skull in.

"You never liked me!"

"Why should I? How long have you been sleeping with my husband, Jade? I gave you a job, a house, and a chance," Pandora hissed like a snake, "how long have you been smiling in my face and cashing the checks I write you, all the while enjoying *my* husband in *my* office?"

"I'm not like that," Jade cried, lying through her teeth. Gasps could be heard coming from some of the board members as Jade looked around the room desperately.

"So, you're gonna look in my face and lie further?" Pandora leaned forward, filling the room with a fearsome and pitiless coiled energy. "What about my computer that you've been hacking into? You *do* know that breaking into a government computer is a federal offense. I don't think any of these board members accept medical students with felonies on their records."

One of the board members clutched her chest and slid her chair back. She couldn't believe what she was hearing.

"Pandora, stop this! I'll admit it; I went into your computer looking for a file I needed to print out. I should have asked, okay? But I didn't sleep with your husband! I have the utmost respect for you. Why would I—"

Pandora held her hand up to stop her in mid-sentence, growing tired of Jade's lies. She stood up, grabbed her purse and reached inside, pulling out pictures of Jade and Jackson sleeping together all throughout Pandora's office and scattered them across the conference room table. Jade screamed to the top of her lungs, nearly passing out from the embarrassment.

"*Like I said*, you've been sleeping with my husband."

Shocked responses from Dwayne and the rest of the board members filled the room. Many of them dropped their pens and stood up.

"I think this interview is over," one of the members dropped Jade's file in the nearest trash as he grabbed his things in anticipation to leave.

Jade snatched her belongings and rushed to the door, stopping in front of Pandora. "I swear, you belong in hell with the devil and his demons!"

"Oh honey, there's no devil in hell. *I'm right here in the flesh,*" Pandora's face was hard as stone. She looked like a mixture of poison and pure fire. "You now have *fourteen minutes* to gather your belongings and get the hell out of my city, or I will have the federal government drag you to jail," she glared with eyes full of deadly promise.

Jade turned and stormed out of the office, rushing past Lauren who had been watching everything from the window in a sheer terror.

As the board members began to disburse, Pandora walked over to Dwayne.

"Is it done?" She tilted her head and raised an eyebrow.

"It's done," Dwayne rubbed the back of his neck and nodded. "If I get caught, that's first-degree murder, *Anna.*"

"And you'll be in another country where United States laws and jurisdictions don't mean a thing."

Dwayne thought for a minute before shaking his head. "You're a really effed up individual for this."

"All I did was set the trap. *She* stepped on it," Pandora smiled. "By the way, I hear Africa is a beautiful place to call home. Your money will be waiting for you when you get there."

"Right," Dwayne responded, remorsefully.

"It's been a pleasure doing business with you. *Totsiens.*" She winked, wishing him a fluent goodbye in an African tongue.

Pandora spun around and strutted out, leaving Dwayne standing there with a face full of regret. Pandora reminded him of the time he'd seen a tigress hunt a deer while he was in India one summer. The tiger's dappled coat was sunrise-orange with bat-black stripes. She had a lumpy, blocky head with large, carnivorous incisors. With a mighty leap, she sprung upon the shell-shocked deer. A snarl, a rip, a grunt of satisfaction and it was over. *Veni. Vidi. Vici.*

An hour later

Jade sat in the waiting room of the medical clinic with Lauren awaiting their test results. Her life had just turned upside down in ways she'd never believed were possible. How did this happen? Where was Jackson? And what all did Pandora know? Jade was ready to follow orders and hightail it back to Chicago, but Lauren insisted she stay with her.

"Listen, after this, we'll go get your things and head back to my house until this all gets sorted out."

"Hell no," Jade looked at Lauren like she was crazy. "After this, I'm gone. I don't want any part of that psycho."

A nurse technician came out of the office. "Harris. You can come back in now."

Jade got up and wiped her face as best as she

could, but she couldn't stop the tears from falling. Lauren tried rubbing her back, but Jade juddered away and walked into the office.

"Is everything okay, Miss Harris?"

"No. I'm really pressed for time, can you just give me my results so I can get out of here," Jade sat down in the office chair.

"Sure," the woman sat down and grabbed her clipboard. "Now, before we get started, I want to talk to you about safe sex and the dangers of not using protection. Are you sexually active, Miss Harris?"

Jade sighed. "Yes."

"How many sexual partners have you had in the last month?"

"Just one," Jade said impatiently, looking at her watch. "Look, I really just came here to support my friend. I use condoms. I've slipped up once, maybe twice, but for the most part. I know what I'm doing."

"Well, you do know that one slip up can—"

"Lady!" Jade sat forward. "Seriously. Come on."

The woman looked down at her clipboard shaking her head.

"Congratulations, your chlamydia, syphilis, and gonorrhea tests were all negative," the woman looked up with a serious face. "Now, before I give you your HIV results, it's protocol that I let you know the importance of safe sex and the risks of HIV, otherwise I can't release your file.

Jade flung her hands into the air and slammed herself back into the chair. The counselor smiled and proceeded to talk for five minutes about the prevalence rates and risks for AIDS, and how people living with the disease have gone on to live with the help of medication and healthy lifestyles.

"Oh my God, *please* just give me the results! You have no idea of the trouble I'm in right now," Jade snapped.

"Miss Harris, you are HIV positive," the counselor responded.

Jade   fainted   in   the   office.

Chapter 14

Welcome to the Karma Café. There are no menus.
You will get served what you deserve.

Bruce sped down the highway, dipping in and out of traffic like he was auditioning for NASCAR. He'd received a phone call informing him that Pandora was down at Drinkers in the process of getting Jackson released from prison on bail. With the type of charges Jackson was up against, posting bail was unheard of. This sounded like the workings of a good lawyer, but there was no way Pandora could be the one to represent Jackson due to a conflict of interest. Five minutes later, Bruce sped into the prison gates and swerved into a parking spot, nearly smashing into a parked police van in front of him. He jumped out and stormed into the building like a swarm of angry bees, just in time to see Pandora at the front desk with her back turned, filling out paperwork.

"What the *hell* are you doing, and how the hell are you doing it?" He barked, slamming the door behind him.

"It's nice to see you too, Bruce," Pandora never bothered to turn or look up from her paperwork. She knew someone would eventually summon Bruce before she could get in and get out.

"Nice of you to resurrect yourself after six weeks of ignoring me," he walked up behind her.

"Just like it was nice of you to pop up at my house and drive my husband out of it in *handcuffs*," she spun around with darting eyes. They both stood face-to-face, invading one another's personal space.

"I was doing my job," he gritted.

"Are you *really* doing your job, Bruce? Or are you working overtime to get rid of my husband to ensure you get what it is you *really* want?"

Bruce raised his eyebrows and tilted his head. "Are you kidding me right now?"

Pandora pursed her lips and folded her arms.

Bruce lowered himself to Pandora's eye level and leaned in, just inches away from her lips. "Your cookie isn't that good to jeopardize my career."

"I beg to differ," she whispered with a smug grin.

They both glared at one another, filling the waiting lounge with a poisonous energy. Sweat began protruding from Bruce's forehead as he stepped back and grimaced.

"Joanna, I'm serious. *Leave,* or I'll arrest you for intrusion and put you in a holding cell until this all blows over."

"*Try it,*" Pandora threatened. The slits in her eyes looked like razors. "I'll have you charged and sentenced for false imprisonment and unlawful restraint before you can grab your cuffs from your back pocket. I'll see to it that the government has you dragged out of here, along with the end of your career."

"You wouldn't dare."

"You wanna dance? *Let's dance*," Pandora looked like poison, there wasn't a trace of heart in her eyes.

"Whether you want to believe it or not, your husband is *guilty*! All roads point to him. I got a statement from Ashley Peterson and two guards who have seen him coming in and out of that prison to see her over the last three years. I have—"

"No. What you *did* was get a statement from a criminal who committed capital murder; a former client of mine who's case I failed to win, and now it appears she's trying to sabotage my life, and you're falling for it." The anger in her voice elevated.

"Whatever...Jackson has been sneaking around with that woman long before he knew you existed. He's the reason she went nuts in the first place."

"I read the file," Pandora moved closer and got in Bruce's face. "Did you ever think that maybe Ashley could be trying to set Jackson up?"

"*Oh my gosh*," Bruce flung his hands in the air. "You can't be serious right now."

"I'm serious as a heart attack. There are so many other people that need to be looked at under a microscope! You want to lock somebody up for murder? How about you go after *Jade*. She and Travis were lovers the entire time. Everything about that whore is a bald-faced lie. Is it unthinkable that Travis falling in love with Eden could have pissed her off and caused her to start all of this?"

Moving his body into Pandora's, Bruce roughly backed her into a wall. "You know damn well that's not the truth!" He yelled at the top of his lungs.

"My husband may be a lot of things," Pandora pushed him out of the way and moved to a safer distance, "but he's not a murderer. His baby died right along with Ruby. The baby he fought for and begged Eden on bended knee to be a part of her life. The baby he cut our wedding short over and raced back into the city from Puerto Rico to witness her birth. The same baby that, when he found out she died, he almost had a heart attack in the emergency room."

The door to the back slowly opened and Jackson made his way out, being followed by a warden and the attorney Pandora had paid to take on his case.

"Anna," Jackson frantically called as he rushed over to her with a confused, terrified look on his face. He gripped her into his arms and held on to her as tight as he could.

"You enjoy the light of day," the warden snorted. "Your wife won't be able to save you much longer."

"Is that all, sir?" Jackson's attorney stated with an attitude.

The warden and Bruce looked at Jackson's pitiful, guilty face as he hugged his wife and she bought right into it. They could see right through him. The Warden shook his head and disappeared back into the prison.

"You can't be this blind," Bruce shook his head, staring at Pandora like she had three heads and six arms. "He's gassing your head up, and *you* of all people fell for it."

"Don't play with me, Bruce!" Pandora let go of Jackson and turned to face him one last time.

Bruce was so disgusted it took everything in him

not to spit in Pandora's face. Angry as an earthquake, he stormed out of the building muttering profanity that hadn't even been invented yet. Jackson, Pandora, and Jackson's attorney walked out of the building into the parking lot where Pandora's car was parked.

"I'll be in touch," Jackson's attorney stated.

"Absolutely, thank you so much for doing this for me, Josh."

"No problem. Anything to help out a friend," Josh smiled. "We'll get to the bottom of this soon."

"I appreciate it, man," Jackson's voice shook as tears rushed to the surface of his eyes.

"No problem," Josh patted Jackson on the back. "Stay strong and lay low. You'll be fine." Josh turned and walked away.

Pandora got into her car and Jackson followed. The second both of their doors were closed, Pandora turned to face Jackson.

"What in the *hell* did you d—"

"*You* did this!" Jackson blurted out before she could finish. Big, crocodile tears instantly fell from his lying face.

"Excuse me?"

"*You* and Quinn bought that murdering psycho Jade back here and she framed me. I shot Travis for what he did to Eden, and she was bent on making me pay for it. She's jealous of you and she hates Eden, so she used me as a pawn to do her dirty work."

Pandora's car keys fell from her hands and her mouth fell open. She knew Jade was behind this the entire time.

"Listen, I went out one night with the guys after work and I got drunk. She was there and ended up taking advantage of me. She took pictures, videos, the whole nine. I didn't even know it until she started emailing them to my work email as threats. She told me she'd rat me out if I didn't help her, so I did," he cried. "I'm not sure what she was after but she kept hacking into your computer and using me for sexual favors." Jackson's puppy dog eyes gazed at Pandora as he caressed her face. "Baby, I don't know how I got dragged into this but I'm not a… I didn't kill anybody."

Pandora couldn't believe that so much had been going on right under her nose and she had no knowledge of it. Now, everything was *one big mess*, and it would cost her everything to sort it out.

"I believe you."

"All I've ever wanted was you. I don't know where these accusations are coming from. I didn't mean to cheat, Anna. I swear to you. I was drunk."

"I said I *believe you*," her voice shook as she put her hand up to stop him from repeating his sentence.

"And then they used Ashley Peterson to frame me!" He continued. "I knew of her from the case you worked on."

Pandora stared at Jackson for a few seconds before replying. "Did you?"

"I grew up with her younger twin brothers. Because she was much older, I'd never seen her before. I didn't realize the connection until she came up in a discussion."

"And you said nothing to me about it?"

"I just found out this week. Her mother came over to see my mother. Apparently, her whole family knows you put her away, and I'm married to you. It's been one big awkward secret that's been kept from me. I hadn't had a chance to tell you yet."

"Hmm..." Pandora furrowed, as Jackson told a half-truth. He *did* grow up with Ashley's younger brothers, which was how Ashley met him and began cheating on her husband with him. Nobody in Ashley's family knew about it, so Jackson had somebody to vouch for him in the event he needed an alibi.

"Her older brothers just had a set of twins themselves, and Ashley's son just turned thirteen last week. They all live with Ashley's mother and father. Her grandmother, who she's been really close with all her life was just diagnosed with Cancer. Apparently, they're all preparing to go down to the prison to tell Ashley this week, and when her full name came up, someone mentioned your name. The whole house looked at me funny." Jackson shook his head and watched Pandora who stared at the road as she drove. He waited patiently for a reaction, but when she didn't give him one, Jackson started to worry that Pandora wasn't feeding into his deception. He placed his hand on her thigh. "Listen, I really don't want to get you involved, but I need to clear my name. Couldn't we all go to Ashley's parents' house? You could sit down and talk to them. They'll tell you themselves that I knew nothing about her."

"We *could* talk to them*,*" Pandora shrugged, coldly. "But unfortunately the dead can't talk back..."

422 Kensington Avenue, Virginia Beach, Virginia.

Ashley's son, Carlos, sat in his grandmother's apartment by her bedside watching tearfully as she withered away from cancer. At seventy-three-years-old, Rika Peterson was once in the best shape of her life. A few months prior she had just raced for a breast cancer cure, and now she was in need of one. Fourteen-year-old Carlos held his grandmother's hand and cried tears of anger and hurt. Ever since Ashley had gone coo-coo for cocoa puffs and got locked up for life, his grandmother and grandfather had taken over raising him. They made sure he excelled in school and had a nice place to live. Carlos's twin uncles made sure his grades were good and put him in sports. Ashley's family did the best they could to ensure Carlos lived a normal life. They all visited Ashley often, but Carlos hated it.

His mother was his best friend and he couldn't stomach seeing her behind a Plexiglas and talking to her through phones. He was too young to remember the crime she committed, but he heard stories growing up as to why he had no father. Although his family ensured a normal upbringing, Carlos still dabbled into trouble. He hung out with the wrong crowd, skipped school, and smoked marijuana behind his family's back. He even sold drugs here and there when he needed money for the Jordan's his grandmother and uncles wouldn't buy.

"Carlos," his grandmother coughed. "When you go see your mother, do me a favor."

"What's that, Grandma?"

"Smile. Be happy," she begged. "It's bad enough she has to talk to her son from a prison phone. When she hears about my condition, I'm not sure how she'll react."

"That's not my problem," Carlos replied angrily. "Why do I have to spare her feelings because she's locked up? She didn't spare mine when she put herself there. Yours either."

"Carlos!" His grandmother gritted through another gruesome cough.

"Alright. I'll be nice—this time. But after today I'm not going back to see her."

"She's still your mother. You still owe her respect."

"I don't owe her anything."

"You owe her everything!" A deep voice threatened by the bedroom door.

Carlos turned to see his uncle glaring at him as he held one of his newborn twins. "I told you about talking to my mother like that; you need to watch your mouth."

"I wasn't talking to her like anything, Uncle Rob." Carlos stood up with creases in his brows. "I don't wanna go see my mom and everybody keeps making me."

"Come here. Come talk to me for a minute," Robert motioned for Carlos to walk him out of the room.

Carlos followed, closing his grandmother's door behind him.

"Listen, I know you're mad at your mom. Shoot, we all are. She messed up her life over something that could have been avoided. But regardless of how I feel, that's still my sister and I love her. Staying angry at her won't help."

Carlos crossed his arms and rolled his eyes. "You know, I was angry at my mom for years because I thought she treated your uncle better than me. He always got extra love, more money, and fewer whoopings. If I'd known she'd have cancer and her days with my sons would be limited, I don't think I would've spent my life being angry."

"Yeah, but at least your mom is here. At least you can see her when you want."

"Listen, nephew, sometimes you have to play the hand you were dealt. Tomorrow's not promised. If something happened to your mother today or tomorrow I guarantee you'll regret your attitude." Robert gave him a pat on the back and Carlos began to soften up. As angry as he was, his uncle had a point.

"You're right."

"That's my boy," Robert smiled, as his eight-month-old twin son reached out for Carlos to pick him up.

Carlos scooped his cousin out of Roberts's arms and grinned at him.

"We're gonna head out in a little bit."

"Okay. Me and baby Rob are gonna take a walk around the block."

"Cool," Robert patted him on the head. "Just don't go too far. Be back in five minutes."

"Alright," Carlos nodded and walked out the front door with the baby. As Carlos walked down the street, the warm August morning was like any normal day. Trees rustled in the breeze, traffic lights flashed, and pedestrians walked along the sidewalks. The city of

Virginia Beach was always extremely noisy, but as Carlos turned down a corner, something felt different. He stepped to the side as a tall, brown-skinned woman with dreadlocks descending into a ponytail down her back walked toward him. Carlos gave her a quick once over and laughed to himself at her awkward attire. She had black Reebok sneakers over yellow spandex. It was nearly ninety degrees outside and she wore a black cotton trench coat.

"Jamaicans wear anything these days," he shook his head as she passed.

"Excuse me young blood," the woman said in a thick Jamaican accent. "Do you have a light?"

Carlos turned to look down and saw the beady cigarette she held in her hand made of small brown paper. Carlos's dark lips must have been a dead giveaway that he smoked.

"Yeah, sure…" he responded, taking his black lighter from his pocket. He walked back over to her and lit her cigarette. He failed to notice the machete she slid down her trench coat sleeve that dropped into her hand. With one swift movement, she swung. Carlos's eyes shot open in fear as the razor-sharp blade connected with his throat and severed his head. The baby fell from Carlos's arms, and the Jamaican woman swung her blade a second time, cutting the infant in two. Both the baby and Carlos's headless bodies slumped to the ground in broad daylight. Carlos's head lay beside him etched with a horrific expression.

The woman ran into a nearby alley as four other Jamaicans climbed over a nearby gate and rushed into

Carlos's grandparents' house. In a matter of three minutes, they sprayed the Peterson's home with bullets, and ransacked bodies with samurai swords, killing Ashley's mother, father, uncles, and the remaining three babies. When the police and homicide detectives arrived, they walked into a scene that spoke of rage and hate.

The holes in Rika Peterson told of a messy end. After the first bullet to her brain, the other thirteen were pointless. They found Ashley's father in the bathroom with his pants down slumped over the toilet. Police counted at least four bullet holes in his body, and there was one to make sure he was good and dead because the back of his head was missing and splattered all over the wall above the toilet. The bodies of Ashley's twin brothers and their infant babies lay bloody and armless, as if a chainsaw had hacked them apart. Pandora's box was open. *The war was on and popping.*

At the Prison...

Ashley sat in the waiting room of the Virginia State Penitentiary awaiting her family. She hadn't seen her son in over a month, so she was excited when her brother had told her he was coming. Ashley sat in her prison cell for nine years, regretting the choices she made that landed her there in the first place. Ashley knew she should never have gotten caught up with Jackson, but after her husband cheated on her with the maid, she wanted revenge. Ashley always looked at Jackson like a little brother. He was her younger twin brother's friend.

She should have never allowed things to get that far. She'd ruined her life, and now Jackson caused her to ruin the lives of the innocent for a promise that he never kept. All she had left was her son, her mother, her brothers, and two sets of twin nephews that she could live vicariously through. It kept her going on the days she wanted to give up and commit suicide. Their love gave her a reason to live. As she sat in the waiting room glancing at her watch, she wondered what was taking them so long. Had her son changed his mind? Suddenly, the television above the soda machine that had been playing soap operas flicked off and the news popped on.

"Breaking news. A gruesome, bloody and repulsive massacre took place shortly after eight o'clock this morning on the four hundred block of Charter Oak Drive. Police responded to gunshots in the home, only to come find the severed and decapitated bodies of a 73-year-old woman, a seventy-eight-year-old man, two 35-year-old males, and three infants. Just outside the home were the severed heads of a fourteen-year-old boy and an eight-month-old infant. Police haven't released any names yet, pending family identification. The suspect or suspects are still at large."

Ashley screamed until she passed out.

Chapter 15

Man has his will- but Woman has her way
—Oliver Wendell Holmes

Pandora stood in her large, European styled contemporary kitchen, broiling a steak she'd prepared for her and Jackson for dinner. Using an oversized spoon, she stirred the mashed potatoes and corn on the stove until they were just about ready. Playing Suzy homemaker was the last thing on her mind during a time like this, but she needed to preoccupy her time with something to keep her composed. Periodically, she reminisced over how much fun her and Jackson had when they first began dating. While she was a fan of upscale restaurants, fine wine, and exotic vacations, Jackson was the exact opposite. He wooed her with picnic lunches, Netflix movies, and road trips in his father's 1969 truck. She found beauty in his cheesy romanticism and learned how to find joy in the small things.

Of course, he was no Bruce, but he was authentic and real. Most importantly, he belonged to her, and that was never up for debate. She never had to sneak in and out of places to see him, and she could call and text him whenever she wanted without wondering if he had a wife somewhere.

Pandora choked out a cry as her eyes stumbled on a photo of her and Jackson's first kiss. After they posed for the camera, he told her how much he loved her. Although it took her almost a year, she eventually said it back. She smiled bashfully, remembering their late-night rendezvous and early morning quickies before she got her workday started. She remembered their wedding and all the promises they made at the altar.

Pandora and Jackson spent their first anniversary working, but promised one another to make up for it the second time around. This year, they planned to celebrate in Dubai in a fancy five-star hotel, drinking wine and making memories. Unfortunately, the big celebration had come and gone while Jackson sat in prison for murder and Pandora hid out in a hotel three months pregnant with a baby that didn't belong to him.

She shook her head as tears rolled down her face. *At what point did everything go wrong?* She swore after her and Jackson's love lived on following everything that happened with Eden, they'd last forever. Pandora learned the hard way, however, that forever didn't always last. Her mind, body, and soul belonged to Bruce, and the more she denied herself of her guilty pleasure, the harder life became.

Back at the hotel, she warred with her foolish heart and thought back on all the damage loving a man had caused. Finally, she gave up. It felt safe to stay with Jackson and work through her emotions as a good wife should, but well-behaved wives seldom made history. Bruce was who she *really* wanted. They'd fought through so much to be together, but time was never on their side.

Bruce had gone to hell and back for her. They *owed* love a fair chance, and as Pandora massaged her three-month pregnant belly she decided it was officially time to *pay up*.

Still, before dropping a divorce bomb on Jackson, Pandora wanted to help him out of the mess he'd created. He needed a miracle to get off with a clean slate, so she hired the best defense attorney, other than herself to get the job done. *Too bad he'd be dead before he got to see how everything played out.* Pandora took two plates from her cabinet, carefully placing the mashed potatoes and vegetables on them. She made sure that Jackson's food didn't touch because she knew he hated that. Reaching into her satin robe pocket, she grabbed four Percocet from a small medicine bottle. She crushed them with a spoon and mixed it into his mashed potatoes, the gravy mix, and the salad dressing over top of his salad. She wanted him good and sleepy before the party got started.

Pandora always knew there was something strange about the way Travis just appeared out of thin air. She never got a chance to dig into it because Eden went crazy and everything seemed to go downhill quickly after that. After sifting through the envelope Bruce had given her, Pandora still found it hard to believe that her Jackson was the brains behind this entire operation. *Especially* not after the academy award-winning performance he put on after losing his daughter. Pandora ended up doing her own research, and she couldn't believe what she discovered.

When Pandora and Jackson first got together, he had no idea how to fire a gun. He'd come from a modest, religious household that didn't believe in their second amendment. After they got married and moved into their home, Pandora purchased Jackson a 9mm. She tried teaching him how to use it, but his aim was horrible and he appeared to be embarrassed by it so he gave up learning.

Jackson gave himself away when he put a bullet straight through Travis's head with a perfect aim and with a gun that *wasn't* the 9mm she'd bought for him. Pandora found the gun he used and traced it fifteen years back to the gun shop where it had been purchased. The name on the credit card was *Ashley Peterson*. Pandora took it upon herself to look into Ashley's old credit card statements and found video game purchases and dinners for two at seemingly all of *Jackson's* favorite steakhouses and restaurants.

Ashley's husband was a vegan and a doctor so it was very unlikely that he ate steak and found time for video games. In court, it was said that Ashley sought revenge and murdered her husband in cold blood because he cheated on her. It seemed as if she was cheating too; with her brothers' fifteen-year-old best friend...*Jackson*.

Everything made sense after that. Pandora always knew she was great in bed, but apparently, Jackson thought she was to die for. Once upon a time, she prided herself on giving her husband a second Corinthians kind of love, but now he was about to get Tina Turner's, *What's Love Got To Do With It*.

The nerve of him to think he could play such deadly games with a woman who could play better, she thought.

"Smells good in here!" Jackson walked into the kitchen.

Pandora smiled sweetly as she grabbed a steak knife and began cutting through the medium well steak she'd taken from the oven.

Jackson walked over and slid his arms around Pandora's waist from behind, kissing her cheek. "Here, let me finish that for you." He reached for the knife. "What's the occasion?"

"Just dinner, baby." She gently handed over the knife. He was lucky she wasn't in the business of stabbing people because his ass would have gotten it.

Jackson put the steaks on their plates, and Pandora carried them over to the table.

"You want wine?" She asked, reaching for the red Moscato in her wine case above the table.

"After the month I've had, I need more than wine, but sure." Jackson took the bottle and poured himself a glass. "You know, our anniversary came and left this year."

"Yeah," Pandora lowered her head, pretending to care.

"This isn't dinner in Dubai, but it sure feels like paradise compared to that prison."

"I can imagine," Pandora started to eat her food. "Don't worry, we'll make up for it."

"Listen," he reached across the table and touched her hand. "I'm really sorry about all of this. I know you're upset with me."

"I am," she admitted, meeting his gaze. "I can't believe you didn't tell me about Ashley."

"Babe, I told you I don't know Ashley. It's her brothers I'm close too."

Pandora almost jumped across the table after he told that bold-faced lie.

"I swear, I was going to tell you, I've just been really busy."

"You've been *hella* busy," she mumbled sarcastically.

"What was that?"

"Nothing. It's fine. We'll get through it. It's no use crying over spilled milk. What's done is done. All we can do now is fix it."

"Promise me you still love me?" He stared into her eyes.

"Till death do us part," she winked. Jackson missed the threat laced in her voice because he started to babble on and on for the next ten minutes about his month in prison while he devoured his food and chugged down his wine. Pandora was starting to wonder if she'd put enough Percocet in his food because it seemed to be taking longer than usual to work. She would've hated to have to shoot him, but either way, he was gonna die tonight.

After a while, Pandora could see Jackson's eyes growing heavy. He blinked quickly, shaking off the sleepy feeling.

"I saw the news as I was getting out of the shower a little while ago. Someone shot up Ashley's entire family. I mean, not that it's important or anything," he lied. It was *very* important to him. Jackson had grown up with Ashley's family. Ashley was the first woman he ever fell in love with, and her brothers were his best friends. Her family was good to him and took care of him when both of his parents went into the military. He couldn't believe someone would do such a thing.

"I know. I heard about it," Pandora gasped.

"Yeah," Jackson shook his head, trying to hide his emotions. "It was a freaking blood bath. They killed four babies and Ashley's fourteen-year-old son, too."

"My goodness..."

"You've got to be sick out of your mind to kill a child!" He replied, angrily.

"*You would know,*" she thought.

"They were all such good people though, especially the twins. When we were younger, we'd always talk about starting families of our own, and they actually did it. I looked up to them. I wanted that for us one day." Jackson shook his head resisting the urge to cry. "I can't believe someone did this."

"I'm sorry," Pandora replied, emotionless.

"Of course you are," Jackson rolled his eyes. "You could care less. I'm sure after what she did to Ruby, you'd probably want to shoot up her entire family in cold blood like that, too."

"Nah, too sloppy for me. That's not my style," Pandora took a small bite of her steak. "I'm a bit more tactful than that."

"You've killed someone before?" Jackson was taken aback.

"Of course not," she chuckled. "Have you?"

"No," he lied, taking in more of his wine. "What do you mean by tactful?"

"Just what I said," she finished the remainder of her potatoes and put her fork down. "You see, every human dies because the central nervous system gets unplugged."

Jackson's head began to bob up and down. It was becoming increasingly difficult for him to keep his head afloat.

"This can happen in many ways," she continued. "Usually, it happens when either the cardiopulmonary system stops and tells the brain to shut down, or the brain stops, which tells the heart and lungs to give up. In reality, this is a lot harder to accomplish than it sounds. Plus, it's human nature not to check out without a fight, so people are actually hard to kill. A bullet to the head is effective, but stabbings, for instance, are time-consuming, difficult, and messy. Strangling is tough, and folks just don't stand there while they're being axed. Plus, there's too many fingerprints and possible evidence," she gestured with her hands. "If I wanted to get away with cold-blooded murder, I'd probably poison them with Prolactin. It's a colorless, odorless, tasteless substance that's usually given to schizophrenic patients."

Jackson glanced up at Pandora from his plate.

"What's that?" He said hesitantly.

"Prolactin, silly. You know, the same stuff you used when you tried to kill Eden and your baby," Pandora raised an eyebrow and tilted her head with a smirk.

The look on Jackson's face was priceless as he tried to keep his head up. "I did have a bottle to show you, but I poured it all into that wine bottle you've been drinking from," she spoke calmly.

Jackson's eyes widened. Part of him wanted to jump up from the table, but he was having a hard time keeping himself awake.

Pandora stood up and took the liberty of retrieving some old photos that Bruce had come across of Jackson and Ashley spotted together down through the years.

"This surveillance picture is of you and Ashley when you were fifteen, walking into a gun shop. This is the day she purchased that gun you used to blow Travis away with." Pandora placed the photos on the kitchen table for him to see. "And this one is of you and Ashley when you went to go see her in Prison last year. Was this when you were planning her escape so she could kill Miss Ruby?"

Jackson looked at the pictures as if he was trying to focus and explain himself, but the drugs in his system wouldn't allow it. He glanced up at Pandora, and the glare she returned had descended into something that couldn't be described.

"*Checkmate*," she grimaced.

Jackson's body began to tremor slightly. He sat back in his chair with eyes the size of saucers trying to catch his breath and get his bearings straight.

"Anna, what the hell did you do to m…" was all he managed to get out before he went into a coughing, choking fit.

She offered him the glass of poison to wash it down with.

"You're gonna rot in hell for this."

"I'll meet you there in my bikini," she winked with a smirk. Pandora took her seat at the other end of the table and watched as Jackson began to die slowly. She finished her food and enjoyed the scenery as he coughed and choked on his own saliva.

Jackson gripped his neck and fell out of the chair, flopping around the floor like a fish out water. In her mind, Jackson was getting what he deserved, and he was lucky she allowed his own karma to kill him instead of torturing him like she wanted too.

"I'm pregnant, by the way," she smiled, resisting the urge to kick him. "Too bad you're not the father. But, oh!" her eyes sparkled. "Your dead daughter is probably waiting for you on the other side, so there's your chance at fatherhood. I'm sure Ruby's waiting for you too. I hope she *beats your ass*."

Jackson couldn't respond anymore. His eyes started to roll to the back of his head while he gasped for air, fighting to hold on.

"Tell her I said hello." Pandora walked into her kitchen and made herself a bowl of ice cream. By the time she came back, Jackson was lying on his side by her plants, foaming at the mouth. Enjoying her dessert, Pandora took a beautiful selfie with her iPhone and posted it to her Instagram account. After she'd finished her ice cream, she put her bowl in the sink and sat back down.

"We heard from the streets that you were one bad S.O.B," a woman's voice descended from Pandora's basement door. "I didn't believe it. I thought you were too prissy, petite, and educated to live up to your name. But wow, was I wrong."

Pandora turned to see Lilly, the machete swinging

Jamaican who'd killed Ashley's son and nephew, walking over to her. Four other Jamaicans came rushing out of her basement like roaches.

"I knew what we were dealing with when she sent us on a mission to go Texas chainsaw massacre on four generations of women, senior citizens, and children."

"My size and my heels fool everyone," Pandora shook her head. "I like to keep it that way."

"Are you done here?" Another man asked, nudging Jackson with his foot to make sure he was good and dead.

"I believe we are," Pandora nodded.

"Man, PJ must really respect you. That man would kill himself before he sat in prison for *anybody*."

"PJ and I have quite a bit of history. I helped his sister beat a murder charge and relocated her to Puerto Rico to keep her out of trouble."

"That's right, Charlotte!" Lilly responded. "That was you?"

"That was me," Pandora confirmed. "PJ trusts me and knows he has nothing to worry about. I'll get all of his charges acquitted as soon as this blows over. I just needed a temporary alibi."

Pandora was indeed the queen of manipulation. PJ was known for committing messy murders, especially when he made deals with people who failed to live up to their end of the bargain. Pandora failed to show up to his trial on purpose. She wanted a public defender to run his case so he would lose and sit in prison, that way when she murdered Jackson, it would look like revenge from PJ's men, instead of her. Lily pulled out her machete from under her sleeve and walked over to Jackson.

"Here, let me," Pandora offered.

Lily raised an eyebrow at her boldness but handed her the blade. With one swift move, Pandora sliced Jackson's head clean off. Blood splattered all over her kitchen table and floor.

"What do you want us to do with him?"

"Leave half of him here for the police. Send the other half to his mother's doorstep," Pandora replied coldly.

Lilly jerked her head back in complete shock. She'd never in her life met a cold-blooded, vindictive woman of the law before.

"*You got it*. Jason, grab that chair. Lilly, take out the rope." Everyone did as they were told. Robert looked at Pandora. "This might hurt a little bit."

"I'm sure it will. Just don't leave any permanent marks on my beautiful face, or I will come back for you," she threatened, sitting in the chair Lilly brought over.

"I'll try not to." Lilly tied Pandora to the chair and duct-taped her mouth shut. Robert punched her in the face twice, blacking her eye and bruising her jaw.

Pandora squealed angrily, cursing under the tape. The rest of the men grabbed Jackson's head and placed it in a trash bag. Within ten minutes, they destroyed her kitchen, broke her glass windows, setting off her alarm and headed out the basement door.

Forty-five minutes later...

Sweat stung Bruce's eyes as he raced down the street, wiping across his brow with a trembling hand. He was at home making dinner when one of his detective partners called him and told him what happened.

"The Jamaican posse broke into that lawyer's house. Barron just got there and said it looks like one of PJ's doing. He said her husband is lying under the dinner table without his head."

That was the only thing he heard before he left his food on the stove and rushed out of the house. When he got to his car, he realized he didn't have his car keys. He didn't have the sanity to remember where he'd left them, so he took off running like an Olympic sprinter toward Pandora's house.

Is she dead? Did they hurt her? He asked himself over and over again as he ran like his life depended on it. Bruce was never really a man who prayed too often, but during his three-mile sprint, he had the longest talk with God he'd ever had. Just when he thought his legs would give away, he spotted Pandora's house coming up in the distance. This made him run faster.

He gasped for air, and his heartfelt like it would give away at any minute, but he refused to slow down until he made it inside. The second he got close enough to her property; he leaped across her gate, clutching his thigh when he realized he'd cut himself on the barbed wire. Blood rushed down his leg, but that didn't stop him. He pulled out his badge and rushed passed the ambulance and police officers to keep them from trying to stop him or ask him any questions. Bursting through her front door, he saw Pandora sitting on her steps surrounded by police, Quinn, and Andre. Everyone turned toward the door when he opened it.

Pandora's face was bruised and her lip appeared to be busted, but other than that, she was still in one piece.

"Anna," Bruce stumbled across the floor and clutched Pandora into his arms with the little bit of energy he had left, plopping down on the couch.

"It's okay, I'm alright," she hugged him, as he gasped frantically for air. That's all he needed to hear. Finally, everything went blurry and he passed out.

Chapter 16

When the bough breaks...

One week later...

The day of Jackson's funeral had finally come, and Pandora couldn't have been happier. Her brilliant plan allowed her to get away with murder and kept her name from being dragged through the dirt. The police and the FBI suspected that PJ's men had something to do with Jackson's death since Pandora backed out of his case, but there were no fingerprints or evidence left at the crime scene to blame him. Since Jackson was dead, Bruce got rid of all the evidence he'd discovered. The lawyer Pandora paid to represent Jackson cleared his name of any wrongdoing by making it look like Ashley set him up. To the public eye, Pandora just looked like a grieving wife who was forced to watch her husband die. Now, all that was left to do was bury the bastard and she could get on with her life. She walked down the stairwell adjusting her calf-length white dress, joining Quinn and Eden in Quinn's kitchen.

"You look alive and well...in your *white* dress on your way to a funeral," Eden gave her a slow once over.

"Why would I wear black? I'm not in mourning,"

She stated boldly, picking up a pop tart as she joined Eden at the table.

"*Jesus, God*," Quinn mumbled under her breath, shaking her head.

"Anyway, as I was saying before Bridezilla came prancing down here, the only way to describe it is that it was like an out of body experience while I was in my coma," Eden said. "It was like my mom was right there talking to me. She said a lot, but once I woke up all I really remembered was Jackson and Jade."

"Why didn't you say anything?" Quinn asked, confused.

"Say what to whom, Mannequin?" Eden looked at her like she was crazy.

"Us. The police. I don't know. *Somebody*."

"Oh sure, the police. What was I supposed to say? Hi, I just woke up from a thirty-day coma after almost having my head blown off. As I slept, my dead mother came to me and told me what really happened to her, my baby, and myself. Find Jackson, lock him up and throw away the key." She pursed her lips. "They would've thought *I* was nuts."

"Whatever. I would've believed you."

"Not me," Pandora giggled. "I would have thought you were nuts."

"See."

"I guess it doesn't matter anymore. I mean, we can't bring Ruby or the baby back, but the good thing is that he's gone, Jade's gone, Anna still has her job and her dignity, and you're still alive," Quinn replied.

"It would have been nice to have my mom back,"

Eden smiled through sadness. "But after I found out everything, I was kind of happy that the baby didn't live. I don't think I could raise my daughter knowing that her father killed my mother."

"I agree," Pandora nodded. "Let's just promise from now on before we date anyone, we make sure to get background checks and FBI fingerprints on them."

Quinn and Eden chuckled.

"Tell me about it. But what about you, how are you holding up?" Eden asked.

"Oh, I'm fine," Pandora smiled. "Just ready to get this funeral over with so I can move on with my life."

"All you're worried about is a *funeral*?" Quinn winced, leaning against her kitchen counter.

"Yeah, the quicker we get that sick bastard underground, the quicker people will stop sending me fruit trays and nasty food from their kitchens."

"*Right*, because if Jamaican drug lords beheaded my husband in front of my face, threatened my life, and were still at large, all I'd be worried about was fruit too," Quinn said sarcastically as she moistened her lips. She folded her arms and darted her eyes at Pandora.

Pandora glanced over at Quinn and slowed down chewing her pop tart. Quinn was *far* from stupid. The police may have bought into her brilliant story, but Quinn knew her friend all too well and wasn't buying into any of it. Eden glanced at Quinn and then at Pandora's guilty expression. Eventually, she caught on to it as well. A ringing at the door broke through the guilty silence in the kitchen.

"Saved by the bell," Pandora popped up like

popcorn. "I'll get it."

"*Mmhm*," Quinn shook her head. "Come-on Eden, let's head to the church. I have to set up downstairs for the repast."

"I'll see you guys at the church then."

"See ya," Eden grabbed her purse as she and Quinn walked out through the basement.

Pandora walked over to the door and opened it. Bruce stood in the doorway dressed in a double-breasted tapered black suit. Both of their hearts froze when they laid eyes on one another.

"Good morning,"

"Hi," she responded softly as he walked in and gave her a firm hug. Both of them seemed to melt into each other.

Bruce wanted so badly to be there for Pandora over the last week. He knew she'd been going through a lot and all he wanted to do was hear her voice or be in her presence. However, she'd been staying with Quinn since her home was a crime scene and Bruce didn't want to intrude, so he gave her space. Needless to say, he was ecstatic when she called and asked him to be her security at Jackson's funeral.

"How are you?" He let her go and gazed into her eyes.

"I'm fine."

"Have you been home since everything happened?" He shut the front the door.

"I haven't. I've actually been looking for a new place to live."

"Why? I'm sure the county will replace your

broken windows."

"Too much house for me living alone," Pandora admitted. "I'm just gonna sell it and get something smaller." Pandora walked back into the kitchen as Bruce followed.

"That makes sense. How long are you going to be here at Quinn's?"

"Just until tomorrow. I don't want to wear out my welcome."

"There's a home not too far from here. I can set you up in protective custody if you'd like."

"I was thinking more of being in *your* protective custody," she turned and grinned at him.

Bruce's heart almost stopped beating. "Huh?"

"You heard me," she walked into him and put her arms around his waist. "Unless you don't have any room for me."

"Of course I do," he stuttered, hugging her back. "I- I thought you hated me?"

"Why would I hate you?"

"I just—never mind." Bruce had no idea what was going on. He looked up to make sure the sky wasn't falling.

"You hungry?" She asked.

"Sure, you have something for me to eat?" He flirted, watching her swing her hips toward the fridge.

"Yeah. I put some buns in the oven. Will you grab them out for me?"

Bruce didn't smell any food, but he did what he was told. Grabbing a nearby oven mitt, he walked over to the oven and opened it. Inside was a sonogram in a picture frame that read, *Hi daddy*!

Bruce's jaw dropped. He glared long and hard at the scene before whirling around to face Pandora.

"You're pre-you're *pregnant*?"

"*We're* pregnant," she corrected him, pursing her lips into a smile.

Bruce's heart slammed repeatedly against his rib cage. "But-*how*?"

"Well...when two people love each other, they—"

"Come on, seriously. You know what I mean."

"I'm not sure. After the convention, I started to get really sick. I passed it off as nerves. Three weeks later I found out this was why." Her voice shook as her emotions began to take over.

"*What*," he mumbled under his breath. Bruce didn't know what to do. He took the sonogram from the oven and stared at it as if it were a dream. Finally, reality hit him and he looked up at Pandora through wide eyes.

"You're pregnant." His mouth spread into a huge grin. He couldn't believe it. Was this really happening? "Baby, you're pregnant!" He smiled like a kid on Christmas morning.

Pandora softly nodded her head yes. He wanted to hug her, but he couldn't move his feet. Everything else in the room seemed to vanish as their eyes met, sharing a sacred moment.

"I love you," she admitted as tears fell from her face. "I always have and I always will. Everything in my life is so wrong at the moment, everything except you."

Pandora had been hurt quite a bit in her life. But because of Bruce, she'd also loved and had been loved, and that carried a weight of its own. To be fully seen by someone, and be loved anyhow was a miraculous feeling.

"Come here," he spoke softly.

Pandora barely made it over to him before he caught her into his arms like a touchdown pass. *"I love you, too."*

Neither of them could explain why they felt the way they did, they both just seemed to take each other to a place where no one else could. There was nothing more terrifying than true love. It was worth the risk, and they both reached for it. After every breakup, Pandora and Bruce would always find themselves searching for one another in different relationships. Pandora played the fool and allowed herself to be blinded by a prince charming that was really just a charming villain. She risked friendship, loyalty, and dignity in the name of love.

Bruce went through multiple women for years. He got married on false emotions and created a child that ended up hating the sight of him. When that didn't work, he got divorced and engaged again, playing Russian roulette with his heart a second time. They both suffered a great deal of heartbreak before they realized there was no right person, just different flavors of wrong. It wasn't until they came up against their deepest demons, and the unsolvable problems that made them who they truly were, that they were ready for love.

It took a lot of living for them to face the music, but they were finally ready to dance to the beat of their own drum. As they held on to one another, they realized what they'd been looking for their whole life; *the wrong person*. But not just any wrong person: the *right* wrong person. Someone they could lovingly gaze upon for the rest of their lives and think, *this is the problem I want to have.*

Tears surfaced in Bruce's eyes as he let her go and marveled in his reality. Without warning, he lost his composure entirely and burst into uncontrollable tears. He stumbled a few steps before covering his face with his suit jacket to mask his increasingly loud sobs.

Pandora walked into him and put her arms around his Herculean frame. She closed her eyes and all the noise in the room stopped. She felt safe and comfortable, like a perfect dream. There were no more worries, or fears, just a calm, serene atmosphere. It felt like junior year of high school all over again. After twists and turns full of kidnappings, rape, infidelity, children, lies, deceit, failed marriages, and murder, their love story picked up right where it left off in the middle of the Penny Pack Community Park. Love knows no limit to its endurance, no end to its trust, and no fading of its hope; it can outlast *anything.* Love still stands when all else has fallen. *"The race is not given to the swift, nor the battle to the strong, but to he who endures to the end."*
 –Ecclesiastes 9; 11, Matthew 24; 13

One hour later...

Eden stood in the vestibule of Quinn and Andre's megachurch, watching Jackson's family drag themselves down the aisle to bid their final farewells. The church held over two thousand people, and nearly every seat was filled including the overflow rooms in the balconies. Jackson's friends from high school, college, and grad school crowded the sanctuary; his old teammates from track and football were present too. There were guests that flew in from foreign countries that Jackson had done business with, and extended family from Texas to Maine.

News media prepped their cameras outside waiting to get live coverage when Pandora walked in. Eden watched as all eighty-seven people from Jackson's immediate family flooded the aisles from the front of the church to the rear, waiting their turn to see the casket. Jackson had a beautiful white casket that Pandora ordered for him. Because of his severed head being sent to his mother's doorstep three states away from the rest of his body, it was too deformed to be sewn back on properly, so he had a closed casket funeral. Pandora's first choice was to cremate him and flush his ashes down the toilet, but Jackson's mother had a fit and wanted her only son to have a big funeral.

At first, Pandora was adamant about doing what *she* wanted, but in the end, she gave his mother her last wishes. He was going to hell anyway, so it really didn't matter. Tears poured from the eyes of Jackson's mother and sister as they nearly passed out at the front of the church. Pandora stood in the back behind the pulpit in Andre's office where no one would see her. The entire melancholic atmosphere and all the black clothes freaked her out. She refused to go in.

"Anna, you have to at least show yourself in the

sanctuary. You're his wife," Quinn said.

"I am *not* going in that church with all of those people."

"Just go up and show your face long enough for the media to notice. Otherwise, they'll have a field day and say you didn't show up."

Pandora huffed and folded her arms. "Go in with me."

"I can't, you put me down to do the opening prayer and scripture, so I have to go in from the front with Andre."

"Then where's Eden?"

"She's in the vestibule ushering. She didn't want to go in the church either so she chose the lesser of two evils."

"Oh my gosh. I am not walking in that church by myself."

"Come on, I'll walk with you," Andre walked into his office, adjusting his collar.

"There you are. Deacon Brown has been looking for you," Quinn said.

"Sorry, I was finishing up my sermon."

"Are you really gonna walk with me, Andre?" Pandora pleaded with her eyes.

"Of course I will," he replied, "you know I'll do anything to keep you comfortable at a time like this."

"I'll walk her," Bruce sneered, entering into Andre's office, "You've done enough already."

"Will *somebody* just walk with me? I don't care who it is," Pandora replied impatiently.

"Bruce- Bruce!" Andre said, excitedly. "It's been a

long time man, what's up?"

"I'm good," Bruce replied flatly, grabbing Pandora's hand. He didn't want to be around Andre another second. "Come on baby, let's go."

"*Wow*, look at you two," Andre smiled in awe. "You look like the cutest couple photo from our junior high yearbook."

Pandora blushed.

"Thanks. Maybe we would've made it into the college yearbook if you hadn't *slept with* her and ruined it all," he grimaced, unable to contain himself any longer.

Pandora's smile instantly faded and Quinn choked on her spit, nearly coughing up a lung.

"What?" Andre winced, taken by surprise.

"You heard me," Bruce gritted, letting go of Pandora's hand as he walked over to him ready to attack.

"Excuse me?" Pandora stared at Andre and Bruce, confused.

"You were supposed to be my boy, you black, big-lipped, bastard!" With one swift move, Bruce threw his body weight behind the right hook that connected with Andre's jaw, sending him flying into the back door of his office.

Quinn was so shocked, she was incoherent at this point.

"Did you think I wouldn't figure it out eventually?" Bruce hollered, cupping Andre's head into his hands as he smashed his kneecap into his nose.

Blood immediately spilled from Andre's mouth. Andre got up and grabbed Bruce by his suit jacket. He drew his fist back and sent it into Bruce's stomach. Andre slammed Bruce into the back door as it swung open and Bruce fell outside into the parking lot. Andre rushed outside behind him and they both began throwing blows and kicks like MMA fighters. It sounded like a train wreck outside.

Quinn finally broke out of her trance and rushed outside to break them up. "Stop it, now!" Quinn tried getting in between them.

Pandora grabbed Bruce by his arm and swung herself in front of him. "Stop, both of you!" She hollered.

"What in the world is going on?" Quinn fussed.

"Your husband stole what belonged to me, is what's going on!" Bruce yelled angrily.

"I didn't do anything!" Andre tried to defend himself.

"You had your own woman, why did you have to touch mine!?"

Pandora looked back and forth, putting all the pieces together in her head. Quinn looked at Pandora and then turned to face Andre like she could pass out at any minute.

"Andre," Quinn threatened.

"Quinn, he's lying, I swear. Look, we were both drunk, and she took advantage of *me!*" He lied, saying anything to keep Quinn from spazzing out.

"*What!*" Pandora's high-pitched voice rang out through the parking lot, setting off a car alarm.

Quinn turned to look at Pandora. Part of her was confused, and the other part was ready to kill her.

"What the *hell,*" Pandora drew her head back. "He's lying. If you think for one second I would— I would never," she stumbled on her words, unable to form a complete sentence. It almost felt like an out-of-body experience. Was this *happening?*

"Are you really gonna stand here and try to play the victim after everything you've caused?" Bruce looked at Andre in disbelief.

"You're gonna believe your friend over your husband?" Andre grabbed Quinn by the hand.

The sting of betrayal pierced Quinn's heart like a dagger. She looked at her husband, and then back at Pandora. She didn't know who to believe, but *somebody* was lying.

Eden walked around the back to see what all the noise was. She stopped dead in her tracks when she saw Andre bleeding, and Quinn and Pandora in the middle of a staredown. Instantly, Pandora blew into a fit of rage. Reaching into her purse, she snatched out her gun, cocked it, and aimed straight for Andre's head. Eden and Bruce grabbed her and knocked her hand out of the way just as she fired, sending the bullet into Andre's arm. Quinn screamed and jumped back as Andre hit the ground and clutched his arm in agony.

"Are you serious?" Quinn glared at Pandora with so much hurt in her eyes before rushing to the ground to see about her husband.

"Are *you* serious?" Pandora hollered back. "You're gonna believe that lying, crooked ass pastor over—"

Suddenly, every emergency exit door in the church flew open and people began to swarm out of the building like bees.

"A bomb! There's a bomb in the coffin!" A deacon yelled, running for his life. "Get away from the building!"

Pandora's eyes grew big. She forgot all about the time bomb she put in Jackson's coffin that morning just before the funeral home sealed it. After the hell he caused while he was living, there was no way Jackson would be resting in peace on *her* watch. He, and everything connected to him was getting ready to be blown to bits. Pandora was supposed to keep Eden, Quinn, Bruce, and Andre near an exit, but with all the arguing, she'd gotten distracted.

BOOM!

A large blast sounded and flames burst out of the large building. The radiation and the intense pressure created in the air felt like an earthquake had just hit the city; *a strong one.* Fear made everyone quicken their pace, desperate to get away in one piece. Bruce pushed Pandora and Eden into the ground, using his body as a barricade to hover over them. Andre and Quinn dodged behind a brick wall, just making it to safety.

Suddenly, the Mega church passed down to Andre by his parents came crumbling to the ground. Smoke, ash, and glass scattered everywhere. Andre peaked around the wall at the jaw-dropping scene. There were bodies everywhere. Some were alive, shaking on the ground; others were dead, missing heads, arms, and legs. Andre stood up, clutching his arm as he wiped sweat and blood from his forehead. He waited until he was sure the blast had ended and the building fell completely before coming out into the open.

There was a man nearby whose chest was completely open, and another man with blood pouring from his head. A woman sat on the ground holding an infant screaming for somebody to find her baby.

Someone informed her that she was holding her baby, and she screamed in horror, letting them know she had another one that got lost running out of the church. Andre looked dazed and confused at what looked like the apocalypse all around him. There was so much chaos and screaming he didn't know what to do. He walked back over to the wall to help Quinn, but she wasn't there. His eyes gaped open. He knew she was with him when they dodged behind the wall. Looking to his left, he saw Bruce tending to Pandora and Eden.

"Is everyone okay?" He rushed over to them.

"We're fine, thank God," Eden replied, wiping blood from the small gash near her temple.

"What the hell happened?" Bruce fussed.

"I'm not sure, but I can't find Quinn."

Pandora and Eden looked at him.

"She ran with me behind the wall and then she disappeared somewhere."

"I thought that was her to the left of us that ran past a few minutes ago," Pandora pointed to the direction she saw Quinn running to.

"Her office!" Andre's eyes lit up. "It's around the corner."

"She probably went to phone for help, let's go." Bruce motioned for everyone to follow.

Police sirens and ambulance alarms could be heard in the distance, as they all rushed in the direction of Quinn's office. Andre really needed to get to a hospital to see about his arm, but he needed to make sure his wife was okay first. The door to Quinn's office was open and everyone walked inside.

"Quinn!" They all called, but there was no answer.

"She's got to be in here somewhere. She never leaves her door unlocked if she's not inside," Andre confirmed.

Pandora walked toward the hallway and she could hear voices coming from the secretary's office.

"I think she's down here." Everyone followed Pandora to the secretary's office. The closer they came, the louder the voices became.

"It's okay, baby, everything's gonna be okay, I'm here," a consoling voice could be heard trying to calm Quinn's sobs. Kissing noises could be heard in between.

"I told you he was no good. You're better off with me."

Andre almost tripped over his own two feet trying to get to the door of the office. He frowned as he quickened his strides toward the door, determined to find out what the hell was going on. Finally, he swung it open.

"What is going o—"

Everyone froze in their tracks when they saw Quinn break free from kissing Diamond and look toward the door, shocked.

"*Well hello, Andre,*" Diamond raised a seductive eyebrow. "We meet again…"

To be continued

www.ingramcontent.com/pod-product-compliance
Lightning Source LLC
Chambersburg PA
CBHW071255250626
47159CB00004B/1194